NINE LIVES of MOSES
on the Oregon Trail

MARION FULLER ARCHER

Illustrated by GEORGE ARMSTRONG

ALBERT WHITMAN & Company · Chicago

WISCONSIN

Oshkosh

Mississippi River

Missouri River

IOWA

ILLINOIS

Fort Laramie

North Platte

OREGON

Platte River

South Platte River crossing

TRAIL

St. Joseph

MISSOURI

Quincy

Independence

The route of
the Van Antwerp family
from Wisconsin to Oregon
1852

1

Charlotte skidded to a stop in the mud of the lane as Pa, mounted on Greta, splashed toward her from the Plank Road, home from Milwaukee.

"I'm looking for pussy willows," she called, standing on tiptoe to receive his kiss. "Do you think the sun has brought them out?"

"Hard to tell," said Pa, shifting wearily in the saddle. "I didn't notice any as I rode along. March is still young, but you may find a few. Gather them quickly and come in to hear all the news of Uncle Waldo and Milwaukee."

Charlotte turned to watch Pa as he rode toward the house. Not a handsomer father in the whole thirty-one states of the United States, she thought.

Drawing her scarf primly around her, Charlotte pretended that she was her mother in the long-ago days. She was Lottie Bertrand, teacher at the village school in Four Corners in New York, about forty miles from Manhattan. She was watching the new doctor from Holland, Dr. Van Antwerp, ride off, her speller and copybook under his arm. In his broken English he had just said, "Please, Mademoiselle Bertrand, you must be my help! How can I be the best physician the village has ever had, when the village tongue I cannot speak?"

The sun was curtained by a cloud, the wind tugged at Charlotte's shawl, and her foot slipped into the fast-running icy water in the rut of the lane. She was again Charlotte Van Antwerp of Oshkosh, Wisconsin, and Ma would soon be calling dinner—and Charlotte with no pussy willows, and wet, muddy feet, too.

Pulling her shawl around her shoulders, Charlotte picked her footing along the rutted lane toward the pussy willow trees at the gate. As she went, she thought with a little inner skip of pride of all the fun and excitement of faraway places there was whenever Pa was around.

Sometimes when Bert, her brother, was not too busy with fishing or trapping, they playacted together. Bert was the young doctor "fresh off the boat" from Holland, with his diploma from the Medical College of the University of Amsterdam his most carefully protected possession. (That diploma still had the most important place on the parlor wall, above the marble-topped table that held Ma's big black Bible.)

Bert was fifteen, younger than John but almost three years older than Charlotte, yet hardly an inch taller. With his rosy cheeks, unruly shock of blond hair, and square stocky body, he was the one Ma called "Pa's real, true Van Antwerp."

Charlotte shivered: too cold for playacting outside today. She hurried down the lane until she reached the pussy willow trees. They were still bare. She was turning back toward the house, when the scream of an animal in pain made her whirl toward the Plank Road again.

The loud voices of boys and their laughter mingled with a cat's yowls made her dart behind the willows to peer fearfully. Two big boys were trying to tie together the feet of a black kitten. Wiggling, squirming, spitting, the kitten suddenly succeeded in biting the hand of one of its tormentors. With a cry of pain, the boy flung the kitten into the roadside ditch. The two boys sprinted northward.

6

"Cowards!" Charlotte called at their retreating backs as she ran to the kitten where it splashed feebly in the water. Kneeling, she strained to reach the kitten. Finally she gripped it firmly, but her left leg and her long gray skirt slipped into the ditch before she could regain her balance. She hardly noticed.

"Poor, poor kitty," Charlotte crooned. She wrapped the shivering kitten in her shawl and ran up the lane toward the house.

Her wet skirt slapped against her legs. Her shoes squished and oozed with ditch water. What will Ma say? she wondered.

Pushing through the door, Charlotte crossed the room to offer the kitten to her father. "Look, Pa—no pussy willows. A real pussy instead!"

Then she stopped, staring in bewilderment at Ma, dabbing her apron at her eyes. Ma—crying? Rather expect the sun not to rise than expect to see Ma crying! Charlotte looked nervously from Pa to Johnny and Bert. They were standing solemnly and awkwardly beside the work table. It was littered with rolled blankets and saddlebags.

"See, Sharlie," said Pa, speaking hastily and using his pet name for her. "Johnny and I are riding west with Uncle Waldo, out west to California, to find us a better home in the sunshine."

"West—west—west," Ma burst out, and then she had to stop because of a sob. Charlotte watched in distress, her sympathetic face unconsciously imitating Ma's puckered forehead and drooping mouth. Ma controlled her voice and spoke again, "Isn't it ever going to be far enough west, Johan? First, Europe isn't good enough. Then New York can't hold you. Then the hard work in Milwaukee made you sick. But I thought maybe the farm that brought back your health was west enough for you."

Charlotte ran to Pa to shake his arm. She cried, "No, Pa, no! Not to California. Not without Ma and Bert and me. Not to California! That's millions of miles away."

Pa looked shocked. Dropping the saddlebag he had been holding, he grasped Charlotte by both arms and shook her gently. "No, no, Sharlie, not millions of miles, only two thousand—just to California, I said!"

"But why, Papa? We always stay together!" Her voice ended in a sob.

"I'm not sure, Sharlie," Pa said quietly, "how long we'll stay together if I have to live through many more winters of coughs and fevers."

He turned then to Ma, putting one arm around her while he held Charlotte close. "I know, Lottie, my love," he went on. "I know you're not the rolling stone I am. I know you hoped the farm would be the last move. And the farm has been better than being up all night and all day to care for the sick, like it was in Milwaukee. But, Lottie, California is a sunny land, gentle to a man's weak chest. Here I've only this run-down farm for a home for you—and Oshkosh with as many doctors as it needs—you know that. Give me a season to establish myself where gold miners need a doctor. Next spring I'll be sending for you and then—then, we'll live—happily ever after, eh, Sharlie? Just like the storybook says?"

Charlotte shook her head, still unable to trust herself to speak, but the kitten squirmed and mewed.

"But what's wrong with this little one?" Pa exclaimed more loudly than usual, as if glad to change the subject. When he took the soaked and battered kitten from Charlotte, Ma suddenly became aware of the muddy puddle slowly forming around Charlotte, of her sodden dress and mud-caked shoes.

"What have you been doing?" Ma exclaimed. She pushed Charlotte into the bedroom in the lean-to behind the kitchen. "Wading in winter? Really, Charlotte, I didn't know even you were that scatterbrained. Lung fever! Is that what you want?"

Charlotte stripped off her wet clothing.

"Nothing dry and clean but your Sunday-go-to-meeting dress," Ma said. "Mind you don't spill anything on it."

She led Charlotte to a chair beside the kitchen stove. Pa placed the kitten in her lap. He had put a splint on its broken hind leg. He had bandaged an open wound on its head. Then he had rubbed the little animal dry with an old towel until its coat was a soft, glossy black. It was a beautiful kitten with a white bow tie under its chin, and four white socks. Full of warm milk that Bert had fed it, the cat purred and yawned and blinked, settling cozily on Charlotte's lap.

"Look!" Charlotte exclaimed as she cuddled it. "One eye is green and the other eye is blue. An odd-eyed cat! Isn't that supposed to be good luck, Pa?"

Johnny came down the stairs from his attic room, carrying another saddlebag. He bent over to scratch the kitten between the ears.

"What'll you name your new kitty?" he asked. "California, in honor of our trip?"

"Oh, no!" said Charlotte. "His name is Moses because I plucked him from the waters, just like the Pharoah's daughter in the Bible found the baby Moses."

Moses grew stronger day by day. The snow disappeared from the hillsides and pastures. Lake Winnebago sparkled blue and ice free in the sun. The roads were firm again.

March was not quite two weeks old when Pa and Johnny prepared to ride off to join Uncle Waldo for the 1852 Oregon Trail rendezvous on the Missouri River.

"Don't be plaguing Mamma with needless pranks," Pa warned Charlotte as he kissed her good-bye.

Then he solemnly unfastened his watch chain. He put

10

the big round gold watch into Bert's hands.

"You are going to be the man of the farm for your mamma," Pa said. "A watch you'll be needing. Wind it faithfully and it will serve you well till we meet again."

A lump rose in Charlotte's throat as she watched Pa and Johnny ride down the lane to the Plank Road and out of sight to the south. She kept remembering all the tales she had heard of towering mountains blocking the trail to California and Oregon. Blistering deserts lay in the way, she remembered. Indians on the warpath . . . a whole wagon train of people starving to death in a snowstorm.

Perhaps it was a good thing in those late March days that Ma and Charlotte and Bert were busier than they had ever been, as they clumsily attacked the farming problems Pa and Johnny had done so well. They fell asleep at night, too weary to spend time worrying.

Neighbors who had never called before came up the lane, curious to see how one woman and two half-grown children could manage the farm. Ma had short, firm answers for the curious ones.

On the last day of March, Mrs. Pennywell, from the farm next north on the Plank Road, came with a jar of her best gooseberry jam and the latest *Oshkosh Democrat*. Ma stirred up the fire, started tea to brew, and put out a plate of pound cake before she took off her apron and sat down to talk to Mrs. Pennywell. Charlotte sat in the south window, knitting awkwardly over Moses, curled on her lap.

As soon as Mrs. Pennywell was settled in Pa's rocking chair, Moses jumped from Charlotte's lap to Mrs. Pennywell's ample one. Without losing a syllable of chatter, Mrs. Pennywell settled Moses securely. Balancing her cup agilely with one hand, she stroked Moses with the other. His contented purrs were added to the other happy sounds in the room: wood snapping in the stove, the rhythm of Mrs. Pennywell's rocking, the boiling of the teakettle, and the rise and fall of neighborly voices.

"Look!" Mrs. Pennywell said, waving the folded newspaper. "Here on page three is a letter from Mr. Masterson who left Oshkosh last spring to cross the plains with a covered wagon train. Settled in a place called Pleasant Hill, Oregon. Now, isn't that a nice, homey name? Just listen to this," she went on, laying the paper softly on top of Moses. "He says right here, John Masterson does, 'This country is without doubt one of the most fertile under the sun. Grass begins its second growth the end of August, and it grows all winter.' See, dearie, it's just the place for a man with a weak chest. And listen to this, will you? 'Demand for produce at the mines down in California is so great that everything brings a good price.' See there! He'll make your fortune, that he will. And listen to this, 'Vegetables are finer than anywhere in America. Women are extremely scarce and highly prized!' How do you like that? Sounds just like John Masterson, Mr. Pennywell said."

Mrs. Van Antwerp poured second cups of tea. Mrs. Pennywell took a long sip. Tapping the newspaper for emphasis, she went on: "From May second to September twenty-sixth they were on the way, he says, but look what they have once they're there. I told Mr. Pennywell just last night, I says if I wasn't so old and set in my ways, I'd just pack up and go along when the little doctor sends for you. My bones could stand a nice, mild winter like that."

When Mrs. Pennywell had gone Ma said, "Bless her. California is a long way from Oregon, but just the same she did lighten my heart."

Spring decided to stay at last. The ground dried out so that Bert could plow the field and sow the wheat. Charlotte was proud of his field, but Bert fretted because it did not look as smooth as when Johnny held the plow. Moses shared Charlotte's delight in the fresh furrows. He followed along after Bert and the oxen. His jaunty tail quivered with excitement as he pounced on scurrying bugs, worms, and even trickles of moist dirt.

While Moses nosed everywhere around sheds, chicken houses, pigpens, and barn, Lottie Van Antwerp planted little boxes of cabbage seeds and onion sets in the sunny south window. She'd set the plants out in the garden when the earth was warmer.

On the last Sunday of April the Van Antwerps gladly accepted the invitation of the Brewsters, who lived on the first farm down the Plank Road toward Fond du Lac, to ride in to Oshkosh to church. Nip and Tuck, the oxen, were too slow for trips to town, so the Van Antwerps had stayed at home since Johnny and Dr. Johan had ridden away with the horses.

Until the bend where the Plank Road followed the gently curving lakeshore, Charlotte kept looking over her shoulder, afraid Moses might try to follow them and be lost. No small black cat appeared, however, so Charlotte settled down between the Brewster boys to enjoy the trip.

It was such a lark to ride along at a good clip on the Plank Road that Charlotte had a hard time preserving the proper Sunday dignity. In church she primly folded her hands and remembered not to swing her feet during the long sermon.

After church while Ma and Bert stood with the other farmers discussing the wisdom of planting flax for a cash crop, Charlotte wistfully listened to the women talking about Mrs. Whipple, who used to live upriver at Algoma. She had taken her five children in two covered wagons and had gone to California to join her husband.

"Why don't we do what the Whipples did?" Charlotte asked when they were back home.

Mrs. Van Antwerp was lighting a fire to reheat the dumplings and chicken. Charlotte poured milk and spooned Mrs. Pennywell's gooseberry preserves into the tart shells baked yesterday. She had to step carefully, for Moses, lonely after his solitary morning, was wrapping himself around her ankles, purring joyfully.

"What did they do?" Ma asked absentmindedly.

"Oh," Charlotte said, "they went to California to find their father. Please, Ma?"

Ma shook her head. Her tightly-pursed lips warned Charlotte not to argue. When dinner was ready, Charlotte sat quietly through grace, but she could no longer resist. "Why, Ma? Why can't we load up and go find Pa?"

"Because I think your pa had it figured out right," Ma said emphatically. "We'd just be a burden to him out there until he gets settled. Bert and I are going to Oshkosh tomorrow to see about getting flax seed. It will give us an extra cash crop, and we can go to California next spring with some money set aside to surprise Pa."

Blinking back tears, Charlotte poked a piece of chicken with her fork. Ma's good chicken and dumplings, usually Charlotte's favorite meal, tasted like unsalted mush today. Charlotte felt a gentle tug on her skirt. Pretending to ignore Moses, she pushed a piece of chicken so hard that it slithered off the plate.

"Oh, dear!" Charlotte murmured as the piece of chicken

conveniently fell over the edge of the table. She felt Ma's accusing eyes on her, so she ate quickly. Moses gulped the fallen morsel and tugged at her skirt for more.

All that Sunday the sun beat down with too much heat for early spring. When the chickens and the animals had been fed and settled down for the night, Mrs. Van Antwerp stood beside the back steps, frowning as she watched unseasonable thunderclouds forming high over the eastern shore of the lake. Charlotte sat on the top step stroking Moses, who was sprawled on the stoop to find relief from the heat.

Watching her mother's face, Charlotte asked, "You can't go to Oshkosh to buy seed if it storms, can you?"

"Planting should be done first week in May," Mrs. Van Antwerp said wearily. "But I don't like those clouds—not at all."

Her mother was too preoccupied to notice that when Charlotte climbed the attic stairs to bed she carried Moses, limp and lazy with sleep. Charlotte knew her mother disapproved of the cat's sleeping with her, but it was lonely in the attic since the boys' room on the other side of the partition was empty. Now that Bert was responsible for the farm work, he slept on a cot in the kitchen. With Moses purring at her feet, or even nestled on the pillow close to her, Charlotte no longer noticed strange sounds that filled the night when she was alone in the attic.

It was stifling and hot in the attic. Moses stretched out on the foot of the bed, and Charlotte knew from the companionable weight on her feet that he was there. She had dropped down, fully clothed, to rest for a moment. But the moment stretched on and on, and Charlotte never roused herself to undress.

15

It was the early morning light that wakened Charlotte. It made her think of skim milk, blue and thin compared to the creamy warmth of sunshine at noon. Moses nipped at the tip of her earlobe and she rolled over, wide awake.

Her sleep had been troubled, and her dress felt tight and uncomfortable. Now she was aware of something else: the wind had begun to scream around corners of the house, lunging with violence at one moment, then lulling to an unearthly stillness. Then the blast would come again, shrieking with renewed intensity at the house. The roof seemed to be lifted up and then settled down again.

Charlotte shivered, from fright, not chill. Hugging Moses tightly, she looked uneasily at the bare rafters and the roof above her. Moses, never willing to suffer restraint long, squirmed from her arms. He ran to the narrow window in the south wall. Stretching tall on his hind legs, he looked out. His ears flattened at the insane, squealing laughter the wind made around the chimney. His tail swelled like a squirrel's plume. The hair along the length of his back bristled, and then he seemed to grow to twice his natural size as his entire fur rose. In the eerie silence between puffs of wind Moses growled deep in his throat. As the wind rose again, shrieking and rattling at the window, Moses turned and streaked across the room to Charlotte. He climbed to her shoulder and cowered, trembling, with his head under her chin.

16

"Whatever is out in the yard to frighten you?" Charlotte asked. Holding his tense, trembling body, Charlotte jumped from the bed and ran to the window.

A quick glance to the yard showed Charlotte nothing, no one to frighten Moses. She swayed slightly in the next gust. The wind was stronger here at the window than it had been when she was in bed. Lifting her eyes to the cloud-covered sky, she watched inky-black, roiled clouds, tinged at the edges with sickly green. They scudded northeastward across the sky at a terrific speed, to obscure the sun before it could climb above the lake.

Charlotte's eyes followed southward along the wind-battered sky—and then she began to tremble like Moses. In the southwest, the wind was sucking greenish-black clouds together and downward into a tapering funnel that traveled toward her, sometimes touching ground with the point of its finger, sometimes bobbing and dipping along just above the ground.

When the funnel touched ground, a shower of dust spurted out behind it, or a tree crumpled under that ruthless finger. And always, in this rising shriek and howl of wind, that funnel cloud with its cruel, destroying finger was coming closer and closer.

"Mamma! Mamma! Bert!" she screamed, crossing to the stair door. Tug mightily as she could, she could not open the door against the vacuum caused by the powerful wind outside.

She must rouse Mamma and Bert before the cyclone reached them and destroyed the house! She ran back to the window. In one of the still, breathless moments she was able to open the window and step out onto the roof. Moses dug his claws into her dress and butted his head closer under

17

her chin as she sat on the roof and slid down. On this side the shed roof sloped nearly to the ground, where the root cellar was built into the hillside. She reached the ground. Giving no notice to the scratches on her bare legs from the rough shingles, she ran toward the kitchen door, screaming against the shriek of the wind, "Mamma! Bert!"

She ran with full force into her mother, whose long nightgown blew around her as she raced toward the cellar door. She grasped Charlotte with her free hand, for in the other she carried Pa's handsome medical diploma from the University of Amsterdam.

Bert bounded from the kitchen door, the big black Bible clutched under one arm, Pa's heavy round watch held in his hand. Tears streamed down his face. "Sharlie's not in her bed!" he cried. Then his voice trailed off in relief as he saw his sister.

Charlotte was thankful that it was only a few feet to the sunken door of the root cellar. She could not have covered a greater distance in the buffeting wind. In the moment that she paused while Ma struggled to jerk open the door, Charlotte buried her face in the deep, soft fur of Moses' heaving side. She could not bear to look at that threatening, speeding finger of cloud. Ma pushed her down into the root cellar. It was strangely quiet in the hole that seemed miles away from the noise and terror outside. The musty air was heavy with the fragrance left by potatoes, beets, carrots, turnips, and parsnips stored there in the fall and eaten long ago for winter meals.

Bert jumped down beside her, awkward because his outstretched hands guarded the Bible and watch, the two family treasures. Ma followed him, stooping low as the door slammed down, closing them in.

18

In the few moments they were catching their breaths, the wind seemed to pause to catch its breath, too. Suddenly there burst forth over them a medley of all the hideous sounds Charlotte had ever heard—crashing, cracking, thudding, splintering, and always the shriek of the wind. Once Charlotte thought she heard a pig squeal and the frantic cackling of hens. She buried her face against Moses, thankful he had been with her instead of hunting all night in the field.

At last when Charlotte thought she could not stand it any longer all was suddenly still. It was so quiet in the darkness of the root cellar that Charlotte wondered in a moment of panic if Ma and Bert were still there. Then Moses dug his claws deeply into her shoulder, Bert sneezed, and Ma gave a wavering "We-el-l!"

In a moment Charlotte heard her mother fumbling with the heavy door. Another moment and the door fell back on the ground, open, and the orange light of sunrise shone in their faces. Bert sneezed again and Moses relaxed his claws from Charlotte's shoulder and cried "Mer-wowl!"

Scrambling awkwardly out of the root cellar, Ma, still clutching Pa's diploma, reached a helping hand to Charlotte and then to Bert.

The wind met them, gentle and balmy now, and cooler than it had been in several days, with the fresh coolness an April wind should have. To the east, black storm clouds piled high, gray trailing wisps hinting at the destructive finger that had just passed by. The sun was warm and bright, climbing up its daytime path from the lake as if nothing out-of-the-way had happened.

The three emerging from the root cellar barely glanced at the sky. Near at hand were disorder and confusion where there had been neat, uncluttered dooryard and barnyard, blank nothingness where there had been house, chicken coop, and pigpen.

It was as if, Charlotte thought, they had climbed down into their own root cellar and climbed out into another world far, far away. The apple trees were gone. The sugar maple and the pussy willows by the gate had disappeared. Only the oak tree beside the unharmed barn remained of all the trees Pa had tended so carefully.

Driven into the rough bark of the oak tree so far that Bert could not pull it out was a red-green iridescent tail feather from Jacques, the proud rooster. That witness to the wild fury of the storm was the only sign left of the fine flock of chickens that Johnny had tended with such pride. Of the pigs there was no sign at all.

What had been the house would not even make a good pile of kindling. Barn and wagon shed were by a miracle untouched.

Charlotte was afraid to trust her voice, afraid to trust even her body to move. Lifting her eyes slowly, first to Ma's face, then to Bert's, she saw that they were feeling just as empty and helpless.

Then Bert slowly shifted the Bible under his arm, to free both hands. He pressed the stem of Pa's watch that always rode in the little pocket below the belt of his trousers. Slowly he studied the face of the watch as if his eyes had difficulty focusing on anything so tiny as a watch after the fierceness of the wind and the destruction it had left behind.

"Five-thirty! I'm late milking Daisy," he said in a matter-of-fact tone of voice that ignored the destruction around them as if it were an evil dream that would vanish.

Solemnly Bert handed the Bible to Ma. He started toward

the barn, but halfway there he whirled and ran back to shake Ma's arm.

"But the milk pail? It's gone," he cried. His face crumpled, and Charlotte felt tears on her own face.

"There, there," said Mrs. Van Antwerp, patting Bert's arm and hugging Charlotte. "Just have a cry. It'll clear the air a bit!"

Her calm words brought Charlotte and Bert to their senses more quickly than if she had scolded. Charlotte stooped to put Moses on the ground. She had been holding him so tightly that he was squirming.

Bert squared his shoulders and turned toward the barn again as Daisy mooed a protest at the milking delay. "I'll wash out the feed pail and use it for a milk pail," Bert said. "But what'll I do for a pan to strain the milk in?"

"Yes! What?" exclaimed Mrs. Van Antwerp, and her voice briefly betrayed her appearance of strength. After a moment she went on, "Milk pans are not all that's missing. We'll have to make do somehow."

As if trying to gather her thoughts for the massive making-do ahead of them, Mrs. Van Antwerp walked slowly to the place where the pigpen had been. Apparently the little house where the pigs took shelter had been lifted bodily. Only bare ground was left. The chicken coop, like the house, was a mass of kindling. There was no sign of any chickens.

A rumble of wagon wheels on the Plank Road was heard. Mrs. Van Antwerp gasped and hurried into the wagon shed, taking refuge behind the wagon from the view from the road. "Land sakes! Look at me, Charlotte," she said, horrified. "Not a stitch on me but my nightclothes!"

The rumbling of the wheels was muted as the approaching wagon turned into the lane. "Look, Charlotte," her mother called, "and see who it is and shoo them along until we can do something about clothes for me."

Charlotte climbed over the wagon tongue and walked into the sunshine toward the shiny green wagon standing before the barn. It was Mrs. Pennywell. "The Lord be praised!" she exclaimed. Then with "Steady there, Bess," to the horse she climbed over the wheel and ran to hug Charlotte. After a moment she held the girl at arm's length and with horror growing in her eyes she whispered, "Where—? Is—? Are you all . . . that's left?"

Charlotte stifled a wish to giggle. This was certainly no time for laughter and yet with the miracle of it all spread before her, the very fact of being safe with disaster all around made her want to laugh.

"No," she told Mrs. Pennywell. "Bert's milking and Mamma—well, Mamma's hiding in there because—well, the wind blew away our house and her clothes!"

"Lord bless her, the poor dear! I'll take care of that!" Mrs. Pennywell pushed Charlotte aside and ran to Mrs. Van Antwerp, who appeared from behind the wagon.

Talking steadily, Mrs. Pennywell whisked off her own shawl and draped it around her neighbor to hide the nightgown, led her to the wagon, and settled her on the seat. Then she boosted Charlotte into the wagon bed. Hesitating only a moment she stooped and picked up Moses and scratched him between the ears for an instant before she handed the purring cat to his mistress.

She stood for a second looking from Charlotte to her mother before she asked, "How is it you were dressed at this hour of the day?"

Charlotte blushed. "Because I disobeyed Mamma and

went to bed with my clothes on."

Ma turned to smile at her, a wry little smile, and Mrs. Pennywell laughed. "There's a time for rules and maybe there's a time for breaking them, too," she declared.

She turned to help Bert with the milk and then hustled him, too, into the wagon, noting as she did so that he was barefoot and with only an undershirt. Trousers with a gold watch chain seemed ridiculous with no shoes and no shirt.

"We'll have a bite of breakfast, and then we'll see what's to be done about you, your wardrobe, and your future," she said as she backed and turned the wagon around.

Mrs. Pennywell paused several times in the mile that separated her farm from the Van Antwerps' to talk with neighbors who were riding out to see the damage the storm had done. Only the Van Antwerp house had been in the cyclone's direct path. After leaving them in splinters and ruin, the storm had lifted, raged out over the lake, and dissipated in a waterspout.

Mrs. Pennywell hurried Mrs. Van Antwerp, Charlotte, and Bert into her cozy, fragrant kitchen. She stirred up the fire and pulled coffeepot, kettle, and griddle toward the front of the stove.

"Charlotte, lambie," she said, "you just keep an eye on the porridge and the ham slices. I'll be back in time to break in the eggs. Your mamma and I are going through my wardrobe. I must have been about her size before I got stout. Mr. Pennywell is always at me to put those dresses and things in the missionary barrel at church, but I hung on to 'em without knowing just why. And now I know! Just keep an eye on everything, that's a dear."

Standing over the hot stove to turn frizzling pieces of ham and stir the porridge, caramel-colored with maple sugar, Charlotte shivered and tears came to her eyes as she thought of the heap of kindling that was all that remained of home. Whatever were they to do? And Pa and Johnny miles away!

As Charlotte dished pieces of ham on the platter warming at the end of the stove, Mrs. Pennywell and Ma returned to the kitchen. Mrs. Pennywell took the big spoon from Charlotte, and pushing aside the last pieces of ham to make room for eggs, she broke them quickly into the hot fat.

Charlotte turned to look at her mother. In a gray dress from Mrs. Pennywell's slimmer days, with her hair neatly combed, braided, and wound as a coronet around her head, she looked beautiful and reassuring to Charlotte.

At the breakfast table, they had only lifted their heads after the booming *Amen* to Mr. Pennywell's grace when a knock at the door brought the first of the many visitors who came that morning to learn what had happened to the Van Antwerps.

Mrs. Pennywell poured cup after cup of coffee and drew each newcomer into the friendly circle around the table. Later in the morning wives came with their husbands.

Mrs. Brewster had heard of the skimpy state of Bert's wardrobe and brought her son's outgrown shirts, shoes, and stockings.

"Land o'Goshen!" she exclaimed as she poured herself more coffee. Shaking her head dolefully, she asked Lottie Van Antwerp the question Charlotte had been wanting to ask all morning. "What are you ever going to do? I'd be hard put to rebuild from the ground up even if Will Brewster was right by my side. But if Will was halfway across the country like your man is—why—well, I'd just plain give up, I guess."

Charlotte caught her breath waiting for her mother's answer. She stroked Moses so vigorously that his fur crackled each time she lifted her hand. Why was Ma so slow to answer?

First Mrs. Van Antwerp smiled and shook her head at her friend, then she said, "No, Melissa Brewster, I've lived neighbor to you long enough to know you'd not give up." Then she studied her hands clenched on her lap.

Those hands clasped so tightly that the knuckles were white made Charlotte aware that her mother felt as small and lost as she did. "And least of all can I give up with Johan halfway across the country."

Hurry! What are we going to do? Charlotte asked wordlessly within her mind. Moses mewed at the pressure of her stroking.

"When you consider that all the livestock the good Lord spared us out of the storm were the oxen and that the wagon was saved," Lottie Van Antwerp said slowly, "it seems plain as daylight to me that we must hitch up and take out after Johan and Johnny and be there as soon as we can to help them set up that home in California."

"Oooh, Ma!" Charlotte spoke so loudly and jumped so quickly to run to her mother that Moses skittered away to hide behind the kitchen stove.

The group around the table sat in silence for a moment while Mrs. Van Antwerp hugged her daughter and patted her shoulder.

Mr. Brewster was the first to speak. "Mighty costly business to outfit yourself for the Californy Trail."

"Costly business to build up right from the ground, too," said Mr. Pennywell. "It seems to me, though that neighbor Van Antwerp figgers to do the right thing, everything bein' as it is. Tell you what I aim to do, neighbor Van. I always have had a hankerin' for that upper field of little Doc's. I'll buy it from you right now. That should give you a start in outfittin' for the trail."

"If that's the way the wind blows," said Mr. Brewster, "I want that lower field, south o' the lane, to try my hand at raising flax, like the *Democrat* was telling. None of my own land is fit for flax."

Mrs. Van Antwerp swallowed before she could answer. "Thank-you seems mighty small for the new start you are giving us . . . but that's all I can say right now. Thank you . . . thank you, Mr. Pennywell . . . thank you, Mr. Brewster, from the very depths of my heart."

27

"Best then that we drive into town tomorrow to the Land Office, eh Brewster?" said Mr. Pennywell. "We'll take care of those two sales before someone gets wind of 'em and makes Mrs. Van Antwerp a better offer!"

Joining in the first laughter around the table that morning, Mr. Pennywell pushed his chair back and stood up. "It's best, neighbor, we get that wagon of yours patched up and outfitted for a prairie schooner and get those oxen reshod. It's many hard miles you have to go before you find the little Doc."

Wistfully the next day Charlotte watched her mother and Bert set off for Oshkosh with Mr. Pennywell and Mr. Brewster riding along beside them. Mrs. Pennywell gave her no time for brooding, however. She set Charlotte to washing dishes.

All that Tuesday neighbors and strangers still came from as far away as Oshkosh to the north and Fond du Lac to the south to hear the tale of the victims of the season's first cyclone. Many women brought gifts of food and clothing. Some shook their heads or shivered and clutched their shawls closer when they heard of the Van Antwerps' determination to cross the wild and dangerous trail to California.

Moses had his share of glory, too, when Charlotte told again and again how he had made her look out the window in time to escape the twister.

Charlotte hardly recognized the old farm wagon when it came up the lane at the end of the day. Its box had been cleaned and loose boards tightened. The wheels had been greased and reset on the axles so they no longer squeaked with each turn.

The wagon box had been fitted with five great bows, one

28

at each end and three at equal distances apart between them. Over these bows was draped a fresh new cover of sparkling white tow cloth. Opened at the front to arch over the driver's seat, the tow cloth covering was drawn down at the back, leaving only a small oval opening, like a rear window.

"It's a tent on wheels, really," Bert said proudly, showing everything to Charlotte. "And more than a tent, it's a traveling workshop, too."

He pointed out the new tool chest fastened to the front of the wagon. A few farm tools too big to fit in the chest were fastened underneath the wagon: a little plow, a shovel, a rake, and a scythe. There were two water kegs.

"We have to carry all the water to drink—and boil every drop before we drink it, to keep us from gettin' the dysentery," Bert explained, proud of his knowledge.

"What's that? It looks like a churn," declared Charlotte, pointing to the little keg suspended between the two water kegs.

"That's just what it is," said Bert, laughing. "No more

working the dasher for you. Ma says we put the morning's milk in there, and the wagon does your churning and come night, there's buttermilk and sweet butter. What do you think of that?"

Charlotte pointed to a wooden bucket near the front wheels. "What's that? Molasses right out in the open? Ugh!"

"Not molasses. That's in a keg packed in the wagon," Bert said. Charlotte eyed him, hoping he was not going to call her a silly girl, as he did too often. "That's grease, Sharlie. See the brush? At night when we stop I'll smear the wheels with grease to keep them running smoothly. The blacksmith said that's the way to keep the wagon running all the way to California."

Bert enlarged the oval opening at the back of the wagon so that Charlotte could look inside. He pointed to each barrel and bag.

"That's flour in that barrel and meal in that one. Ought to be enough to carry us clear to California! Ma bought eggs in town and buried them in the meal, and she's going to add however many Mrs. Pennywell can spare her. And in the flour Ma buried a new set of dishes, just enough for the five of us to start on when we get to California. When we eat up the flour, well, we'll just have to pack the dishes someplace else. Wow! You'd think it would take a century to eat all that flour, huh, Sharlie?"

They stood together quietly for a moment. The hugeness of what had been happening to them made them speechless when they looked at it too closely. Moses jumped into the wagon to investigate, and Bert spoke again more quietly.

"That bag is rice, and those sacks are potatoes. Ma couldn't find many 'cause most everybody's root cellar is empty now. These little bags are tea and coffee and sugar,

30

just for Sundays, Ma said. Here's dried apples and raisins. There's the keg of molasses, right here where we can get it without making everything sticky. Ma says it will take a special kind of housekeeping in a traveling house."

"Ma won't forget housekeeping even when she's traveling two thousand miles, will she?" said Charlotte with a shaky laugh.

"And, see," Bert went on, "the hams and bacons hang from the wagon bows just as well as they did in the smoke-house. Only be careful you don't bump your head on a hambone when you get in and out. And your bed is going to be made up every night, right on top of this chest. How do you like that? Pantry, toolshop, storeroom, bedroom, all in one!"

Charlotte shook her head. "Such a lot of things," she sighed. "It doesn't seem as if the whole house had this much in it!"

"Ho! When you start missing some of the things that blew away, you'll know," Bert said seriously. "Do you know when we rode into town this morning we found smashed in a fence corner something that looked like Pa's old rocking chair?"

Their mother came out on the back stoop and beckoned to the children. "Come along, you two. Mr. Pennywell picked up a map at the Land Office, a map that will take us after your father, clear to California. We're charting our trip, and since it concerns you two as much as it does me, I want you both here."

Charlotte and Bert followed their mother to the kitchen table, where Mr. Pennywell had unrolled a large map. Charlotte saw the American continent, stretched from ocean to ocean. On each coast were dots for towns that showed the presence of man. But Charlotte could not take her eyes from the great central expanse of the continent, empty of any signs of man except for the black lines that marked the trails across the lonely plains and deserts and mountains.

"Seems like most folks make their starting at Independence," Mr. Pennywell said finally after silent moments of studying the map while he rubbed his chin. "I rec'lect right well how John Masterson talked about Independence, Independence, Independence for months before he left."

Charlotte watched her mother. She leaned over the map, her lips pursed, her eyes with a faraway look as her finger marked a path across the map. She shook her head slightly.

"I'd figured it out that we'd pick up the trail at St. Joseph," she said slowly.

"Like I said," Mr. Pennywell interrupted with an unmistakable ring of argument in his voice, "most folks pick up the trail at Independence. More likely you'd get a place in a wagon train at Independence. That's how John Masterson figgered it, and now that I think of it, that's where Mrs. Whipple went—to Independence."

Charlotte looked suddenly at Bert, and she had to hide a tiny smile behind her hand as her mother seemed to grow tall before the bossiness in Mr. Pennywell's voice. Lottie Van Antwerp might appear slim and shy, but both Charlotte and Bert knew from experience that she seemed seven feet tall and mightier than any man when she thought she was on the right side of an argument. And as Charlotte listened to her mother's calm and confident voice, she knew without a doubt that her mother was again on the right side of an argument.

"St. Joseph was where Johan and Waldo planned to pick up the trail," she said quietly. "Somehow, I'd like to follow their footsteps as near as possible."

Holding her left index finger on the tiny dot that marked St. Joseph on the Missouri River, Mrs. Van Antwerp traced a trail with her right index finger slanting across the map from Oshkosh, on the side of the little patch that was Lake Winnebago.

"We'll follow the river valleys," she went on. " 'Twill be easier and less lonesome, too."

Her finger slowly followed the line that Charlotte knew was the Wisconsin River. She paused when she reached the Mississippi.

"We could ferry the Mississippi right here at Prairie du Chien," she continued. "But I'm not sure about roads and settlements and the like in Iowa. So I thought we'd follow the river down to Quincy. Johan and Waldo figured to go to Quincy, too, because Waldo's sister Gertrude lives there and her husband operates a ferry, if I remember correctly. It could be we'd hear news of Johan and Johnny and Waldo right there."

Charlotte stooped to pick up Moses who was rubbing against her legs, purring loudly, but she did not take her eyes off Mr. Pennywell's face. He was listening in open-mouthed amazement to Ma's precise and careful plans.

"From Quincy, as you see, it's almost a beeline across Missouri to St. Joseph. There we can see about joining up with a train that's bound for California."

Cuddling Moses baby-doll fashion, Charlotte rocked him and stroked him under the chin, across the pure white of his bow tie. He purred and stretched up to stroke Charlotte's chin with his velvety paw. Charlotte let out the long breath she had been holding as she listened to Ma's knowledgable conversation about far places and frightening trails.

Mrs. Pennywell chuckled. "Look at that puss, would you!" she exclaimed. "He's going to be mighty lonesome when Charlotte starts off on the trail to Californy."

"But—but—Moses is going, too!" Charlotte said, hugging him tightly.

"Oh, now dearie," Mrs. Pennywell said. "Everyone knows that cats are so attached to places they pine away if you try to move them. They've even been know to run miles back home. You'd best leave Moses here with me."

Charlotte dared not trust her voice, so terrible was this suggestion that she leave Moses behind. Blinking back tears, she turned to her mother.

Smiling quietly, Mrs. Van Antwerp rolled the map and handed it to Mr. Pennywell. Then she stooped and lifted Moses who was running first to Charlotte then to Mrs. Van Antwerp, rubbing against ankles and purring urgently, as if he sensed danger. She scratched Moses between the ears and stroked the silken fur on his cheeks.

"Ordinary cats run back home," Mrs. Van Antwerp said musingly, "but Moses has struck me as being unordinary ever since I've known him. Perhaps it's because he was just a street urchin of a puss without any home until Charlotte saved his life and adopted him. She saved his life, and then he warned her in time to save her life. And so, Mrs. Pennywell, I suspect Moses would run to Charlotte. I think we'll learn what kind of traveler Moses will be."

Charlotte gratefully hugged her mother while Mr. Pennywell rose to do the evening milking. Soon Charlotte heard the empty pails clanking as he walked toward the barn. A plan blazed in her mind. She picked up Moses' saucer from behind the stove and called softly to Moses.

"Every day, every meal from now until we leave I'm going to feed you in the wagon. Then it will be home to you and you'll stay with us all the way to California."

Moses frisked around Charlotte as she ran to the wagon. He leaped ahead of her as she climbed over the wheel, balanced on the high seat, and dropped down into the loaded wagon bed. The top of the little clothes chest was bare, a perfect place for Moses to eat.

Charlotte watched while her kitten attacked the saucer of food. When his first hunger was gone, Moses surveyed the whole crowded wagon bed for a moment. Then he regally stalked to a bundle of blankets stowed under the high seat. There he lay down and started to wash himself.

After a moment Charlotte carefully backed out of the wagon just as Mrs. Van Antwerp appeared in the doorway to call her to supper chores.

The Van Antwerps were glad to accept the Pennywells' hospitality while they finished their preparations for the trail. That last week in April seemed to speed by as Charlotte and Bert thought of saying good-bye to home. But at times the week dragged endlessly, each day lengthening the distance between them and Pa and Johnny.

It rained for three days, gusty showers that were the aftermath of the cyclone. During the wet weather Moses slept in the wagon. "He knows it's his home," Charlotte declared many times. "He's not going to pine away for Wisconsin."

"You'll be pining away from pure uselessness," Mrs. Van Antwerp told her, shooing her back into the kitchen. "I need a good strong stirring arm here if we're going to be ready to leave come May first!"

Mrs. Van Antwerp continued to talk as she tied one of Mrs. Pennywell's aprons around Charlotte's waist. "It's yeast we must make, enough to pack for the long trail ahead of us." She handed Charlotte a long-handled wooden spoon. "Stir this batch while I get this one patted out and cut into cakes. I've heard that some women try to keep their starter alive along the whole length of the trail. But there's too much risk of its spoiling or getting lost. With my mother's faithful old recipe for dried yeast cakes and a good dry crock for storing them, we may carry Wisconsin yeast clear to California. Light bread will taste mighty good after a long day of traveling."

Charlotte vigorously stirred the cornmeal into the pungent batter of potato water, flour, salt, sugar, and yeast starter. Her arm began to ache from beating the stiffening batter. "Mamma!" she exclaimed suddenly. "Our starter—it blew away in the storm, too!"

Looking up from the breadboard where she was shaping yeast cakes to be dried her mother said "Yes?" in a tone that really meant, "Of course, foolish child."

"But that was Grandma Bertrand's starter you'd kept alive ever since you've been a housekeeper. Remember Grandma's saying, 'Bad luck to the housewife who lets her starter die?' "

"By her own carelessness," Mrs. Van Antwerp reminded Charlotte. "Anyway I think we had our year's bad luck last Monday. . . . Mrs. Pennywell let me use her starter, so there'll be the taste of friendship to every bite of bread we eat. Now, you run along and give Moses a big saucer of milk and a plate of leavings to keep him quiet in the wagon. Then you change quickly into your new blue linsey-woolsey dress and brush the dust off your shoes. Mrs. Pennywell whispered in my ear that the good church folks are coming for potluck supper and a pound party for us. It's supposed to be a surprise—that's why I don't want you to look all dressed up—just clean and nice. Mrs. Pennywell, bless her, thought the storm was enough surprise for us this week, that's why she told me."

Mewing with eagerness, Moses followed Charlotte into the wagon to his feeding place. When he was growling busily over a bit of meat, Charlotte pulled on the rope that controlled the size of the pucker-hole at the back of the wagon. If it was small and high, Moses might remain inside the wagon, out of the way of carriage wheels, horses' sharp hooves, and curious church folk.

Charlotte climbed quietly over the wagon wheel, leaving Moses undisturbed with his meal. Far down the Plank Road she could hear the rumble of carriage wheels, the first of the pound party guests, she was sure. In the front bedroom she shared with Ma, Charlotte wiped the dust from her shoes and slipped into the blue linsey-woolsey dress. As she fastened the small buttons down the front of the smooth-fitting bodice and patted the full skirt she thought this second-best dress was almost as pretty as her best dress of red sprigged challis. Two new dresses at once were unheard of for Charlotte, whose new dresses in the past had been made over from ones Ma had saved from her school-teaching days and stowed away in camphor and lavender in a trunk. That trunk was gone, too, probably blown into some fence corner halfway across the county.

Charlotte went to stand beside Mrs. Pennywell and her mother on the stoop to greet the guests. She had never been to a pound party before. Several times Ma and Pa had ridden off to town to a pound party for the preacher when the cash money for the preacher's wages could not be stretched to feed and clothe his six children.

Each person brought a pound of something to help the Van Antwerps along their way: a pound of butter, a pound of lard, a pound of cheese, a pound of cake, a pound of raisins. Mrs. Eastman, the stationer's wife, brought a pound of paper. "So you'll not forget to write us," she said, kissing Mrs. Van Antwerp.

Miss Katie Duniway, the seamstress, brought a pound

38

of buttons of all sizes and shapes. Her sister brought a pound of stocking yarn and knitting needles. Charlotte made a wry face while no one was looking. When it came to turning the heel of a knitted sock her fingers always bungled the stitches.

After the party was over and the last carriage had driven away toward Oshkosh Charlotte woke Moses from his place on the chest in the wagon bed. Buttons, yarn, and dry supplies like beans and rice could be tucked into the clothes chest.

As Charlotte surveyed the wagon so heavily laden with the gifts their friends had brought she thought her family must be the wealthiest in Winnebago County.

"We can eat our way to California and back with all this food," she said. She wondered about the look on her mother's face, half doubting and half worried.

At dawn on May Day, the short-long week ended. The Van Antwerps climbed into the loaded wagon. Mrs. Pennywell brought a crate holding six of her best hens and a fine young cock. The chickens could ride swinging under the wagon. Mr. Brewster brought Tim and Sam, young oxen, as payment for the lower field. Mr. Pennywell helped Bert unhitch and reyoke the oxen, placing Tim and Sam next to the wagon so that old, dependable Nip and Tuck were the lead oxen. When everything else was ready, Mr. Pennywell brought Daisy the cow from the barn and roped her to the back of the wagon.

Bert sat proudly on the high seat, holding the whip. Mrs. Van Antwerp sat beside him, and Charlotte, with Moses on her lap, had the softest seat of all on top of bedding and bundles of clothing at the back of the wagon.

All the good-byes had been said, but still it was hard

to make the final break. At last Bert clucked to the oxen and self-consciously cracked his whip over their heads. The wagon creaked slowly down the lane. Even then, Mr. Pennywell seemed unable to let them go. He strode down the lane after them, grinning up at Charlotte as he walked.

"Sure now you don't want to leave that black cat of yours here with Harriet and me, Miss Charlotte?" he called.

"Oh, no!" Charlotte exclaimed, giving Moses an extra hug. "He saved my life, Mr. Pennywell. I'll never, ever leave Moses."

Off across Wisconsin the wagon rolled, south and westward. In her impatience to catch up with Pa and Johnny, Charlotte wondered why anyone had ever said "snail's pace" to describe slowness. "Oxen's pace" was slower than she wanted to go. Only twenty-five miles on the best days! Bert was impatient, too, and urged Ma, "Let's drive on in the moonlight. Every mile counts."

"No!" said Mrs. Van Antwerp firmly. "Every mile beyond a good workday wears out the oxen, to say nothing of us. Don't forget this trail is wickedly long. Nights and Sundays we rest, no matter how road-hungry you two are."

Beyond Portage they left the twisting, turning Fox River behind. In the last reedy, meandering miles it had not seemed the river Charlotte knew and loved at Oshkosh. As the wagon turned into the valley of the wide, swift Wisconsin River and she could no longer see the Fox, Charlotte felt she was saying farewell to the last link that bound her to her old home.

When the Van Antwerps finally reached the place where the Wisconsin swept out into the Mississippi, Charlotte felt only excitement. To be traveling along the Mississippi made her feel that they were truly following Pa.

Down into Illinois the family went. As day circled after day, Bert mastered the knack of driving oxen. He discovered that Tim and Tuck made a better team, and Nip and Sam pulled as if they had been trained together. Yoking was smoother and traveling better after that.

Sometimes they camped on the bank of a stream. As May wore on and the nights were warm, Bert lifted their bedrolls out under the stars. Ma shook her head, but she no longer objected to Charlotte's cuddling Moses. In the starlit nights, with Moses' head close under her chin, with the sound of a creek or a river in her ears, and with the steady munching of the oxen and Daisy to lull her to sleep, Charlotte loved these camping spots. If only Pa were with them!

Other nights, when lightning struck close to them and the steady crash and rumble of thunder brought sheets of rain, they slept together in the wagon. Then a little black fur piece across her chest made Charlotte restless. She never complained because haunting her mind was Mrs. Pennywell's prediction that Moses would pine away for the farm on the shores of Lake Winnebago and try to make his way back.

There was another night when a farmer's wife invited them to sleep in her spare bedroom. She was lonely and eager to hear news from beyond her horizon. Her husband was off hauling freight to supplement the income of their run-down farm. She and her four daughters clucked in sympathy over the story of the Van Antwerps' bad luck.

To break the boredom of long hours of riding, Charlotte sometimes walked along the road beside Bert. Moses was glad to be freed from the narrow limits of the wagon bed. When Charlotte first put him on the ground, he slunk along, testing with his ears the safety in every direction. Reassured, he galloped ahead, his tail like a question mark. Then suddenly he would turn and rush back to Charlotte, sometimes only to tag her lightly with retracted claws, sometimes to climb on her shoulder.

Charlotte worried when Moses frisked off into a field or woods, refusing to be coaxed out. "What if a wild animal gets him?" Charlotte fretted. "What if he gets lost?" But when the campsite was chosen, the oxen unyoked, and Ma had started dinner, Moses would step softly into camp with a saucy mew.

One day, when it seemed to Charlotte that the month of May was already a year long, she swung to the ground beside Ma, who was knitting nimbly as she walked. "It feels good to stretch my legs and air my mind," her mother said.

It was almost noon and Ma kept a watchful eye on the roadside for lichens to add variety to their usual cold lunch. She saved time by cooking only at night and in the morning.

Charlotte squinted, judging their direction as Dr. Johan taught her by the angle of her short noontime shadow. "South," she complained. "It's ages since we left home and we're still going south. Why, Ma? We want to go west to California, not down to the equator."

Mrs. Van Antwerp laughed. She lifted a lichen from a

tree trunk before she answered. "We're twelve days out from Winnebago County, just a small part of the two thousand miles we have to go, Charlotte. I give us eight more days to St. Joseph. You can start worrying if our pace is slower than that. Tomorrow we should get to Quincy. We'll find Waldo's sister Gertrude. She'll have news of him and Johan and Johnny. At Quincy we'll ferry across the Mississippi. Then we'll be going west to St. Joe. There, daughter, we'll be at just the beginning of the trail. . . . Bert, better pull up at the first good opening. It's time for a bite to eat."

Charlotte groaned inside. A groan loud enough for her mother to hear would have set off a spell of sermonizing, and that always left Charlotte feeling very small and wicked.

Bert guided the oxen off the road to the grassy bank of a little river.

Charlotte helped unyoke the oxen and led them to the river to drink before they were tethered to browse. She took Daisy to the river, and when the little cow had drunk her fill, Charlotte staked her near the wagon.

Then Charlotte unhooked the chicken crate and set it in the grass. "There! Maybe you'll forget you're all cooped up," she said as she spread grain on the floor of the crate and set a dish of water inside.

She went to join Ma and Bert for her share of cold corn bread and lichen. Moses wrinkled his nose and shook all four paws in disgust at the crumbs Charlotte offered him. He disappeared in the tall grass and took care of his own noon meal with a plump field mouse.

All the way down the Mississippi River, Bert and Charlotte asked everyone they met for news of Dr. Johan Van Antwerp. But no one had made the acquaintance of the little Dutch doctor, his tall son Johnny, or his round and jolly friend, Waldo.

They reached Quincy, on its high bluff above the Mississippi, on Saturday afternoon while the sun was still high.

Noting the sun's position, Charlotte said, "We can say hello to Gertrude and be ferried across the river before sundown—and then west of the Mississippi I'll feel so much nearer to Pa!"

"You'll feel farther from civilization than you've ever been in your life," her mother said sternly. "That's what you'll feel west of the Mississippi!"

Both Charlotte and Bert looked at Mrs. Van Antwerp in surprise.

"We're going to camp right here in this meadow," she went on firmly. "There's still enough sun left for us to do a good cleaning job. Bert, you start carrying water right now. Charlotte and I will tend to the animals and get the fire started. When we look clean and respectable we'll go into town—in the morning. We'll find the church Waldo's sister's most likely to go to. Then we'll make ourselves acquainted. We may not have a chance to sit in another church this side of California."

Charlotte and Bert exchanged glances, but they were careful to smother their groans. Ma on a cleaning spree was to be feared and respected! Charlotte joined Bert in carrying water from the river. Soon the oxen and Daisy were grazing and a campfire was blazing to heat the water. Ma washed everything she could get her hands on while the sunlight lasted. Then in the gloaming she superintended baths, first Charlotte's and then Bert's.

When the first church bells pealed the next morning, the Van Antwerps were ready to walk the short distance into the center of Quincy. Bert looked self-conscious in the good trousers and white shirt that had come to him from the next-to-the-biggest Brewster boy. No Quincy lady would be more elegant, Charlotte was sure, than Ma in the gray gown from Mrs. Pennywell's slimmer days. Charlotte herself walked in a dignified manner, to do honor to Sunday and her blue linsey-woolsey second-best dress.

Although Charlotte stamped her foot at Moses, clapped her hands until her palms stung, and spoke far more crossly than she honestly felt, Moses persisted in sneaking after them until the family reached the center of the town. Then he disappeared down an alley after a mouse, and Charlotte's impatience turned to worry.

Mrs. Van Antwerp asked the way to the Lutheran church. "I'm sure that's where we are most apt to find Gertrude Verhoeven," she told Charlotte and Bert.

At the little brown-shingled church on a side street, a man, uncomfortable in a dark suit and high white collar, greeted the Van Antwerp family and ushered them to a pew too close to the front to please Charlotte. When the preacher prayed for blessings "on the strangers in our midst," Charlotte blushed and squirmed so that Ma put a firm restraining hand across Charlotte's hands.

Charlotte enjoyed singing the hymns with the congregation, following the lead of the wheezy pedal organ. But midway through the long sermon Charlotte wanted to rush outside. A loud and hideous catfight began—on the very steps of the church, it seemed. She was certain that it must be Moses accosted by an enemy as he tried to find his family.

Mrs. Van Antwerp must have suspected Moses was responsible for the uproar because her hand closed tightly over Charlotte's. The cats soon became silent, but the rest of the sermon and final hymn were completely lost to Charlotte.

After the benediction Charlotte fidgeted while her mother made inquiries about Gertrude Verhoeven. Neighbors said Mrs. Verhoeven's husband had died during the winter. She had left not quite two months ago for California in a covered wagon with her brother and two other men. Dr. Van Antwerp and John!

Charlotte was cross with life as she walked back to the wagon. All the good feeling that had come to her with the hymns trickled away like water through a sieve. As she stepped along the road searching for Moses, first on the left and then on the right, she became more worried every minute.

"I was sure," Charlotte grumbled as they approached the wagon and the tethered oxen, "that Quincy was going to bring us real news of Pa and Johnny."

"I don't know what better news you could expect at this stage of the trip," said Mrs. Van Antwerp with a glad ring in her voice, "than knowing Gertrude is with them and they're not skimping along on man-cooked meals!"

At that moment, Charlotte saw Moses sitting on the wagon seat, a battered Moses with left ear nicked and right eye, the blue one, swollen shut.

Charlotte cuddled him on her lap, taking care not to touch any of his hurts. The knowledge that Moses made a beeline to the wagon when there was trouble was such a relief to Charlotte that now she was as happy about Quincy as Ma was.

46

Once across the Mississippi the course was almost due west toward St. Joseph, and the Van Antwerps were no longer the only travelers in a covered wagon. The many miles between Quincy and St. Joseph passed with tantalizing slowness, with no one to give them fresh news of Dr. Johan.

Late one hot dusty afternoon they reached St. Joseph. It was really just a little town, not much larger than Oshkosh, Charlotte realized as she looked at the main street. But the Oregon- and California-bound travelers camped in the meadows and on the hillside around the town made it look like a city. The men who walked the dusty streets were not like the tidy, plain farmers and townsmen of Oshkosh.

Charlotte stared. There were men in bulky blanket coats. Men carrying guns, knives gleaming from their belts, were dressed in fringed leather tunics. Shaggy dogs ranged along at their heels. Moses, sitting on Charlotte's lap, stiffened and spat.

Charlotte brushed her face against him. "Shh!" she said. "This is the Wild West. You'll have to get used to people like that!"

"I wish I could call this the West, daughter," Ma said with a sigh.

She sounded weary as she climbed down from the wagon seat. "There's so much West ahead of us, that it seems presumptuous to call this West. My! I'd like to camp right here on the edge of town and go out in the morning, but I think I'd better start dickering for a place in a train right now. We got such a late start that, aching bones or not, there's no time to lose."

Moses, stretching lazily, stepped from Charlotte's lap to Ma's place on the wagon seat. He poised to jump down after Ma. Charlotte whispered, "No, Moses darling. In this crowd one small black cat could soon be lost." But Moses did not take suggestions well. He would do what he had set his nose to do. At that moment, however, a wolfish-looking dog saw Moses and ran at the wagon with a snarl that attracted several mongrels. With fur bristling and tail huge, Moses jumped into the wagon and hid under the seat. The oxen tossed their heads, stamped, and shied.

Bert brandished his whip. With Moses out of sight, the dogs lost interest and trotted off through the crowd. The boy guided the wagon, following Ma Van Antwerp's path.

Bert stopped the oxen when he saw Ma join a group of men and women in front of a store. Charlotte proudly watched her mother, for she looked clean and fresh in her gray dress and sunbonnet. Many of the emigrants had already come a long way, and the women looked travel-worn. No matter how tired she was, Ma always looked proper. Charlotte glanced down at her own crumpled dress and brushed away black cat hairs. Jumping to the road, she joined Bert at the oxen's heads.

"Bert, Ma says this is hardly the beginning of the West," Charlotte said. "And yet do you know how long we've been gone from home?"

"There isn't any home anymore, Sharlie," Bert said. "We're like snails and turtles—we draw our home along with us."

"Oh, Bert, that wagon's not home! But I mean— do you

48

know how long it's been since we left the Pennywells? I've put a notch here on the first bow of the wagon every single morning. I just counted. It's twenty days we've been gone."

Mrs. Van Antwerp returned then, looking very serious. "No one is willing to add a woman and two half-grown children to his train," she said. "It's really too late to be making a start for the crossing, and it seems that there has been a lot of sickness on the trail this year. . . . Oh, dear, I do hope Johan keeps well."

Quietly she climbed to the wagon seat and reached down to help Charlotte up. "There's no place to camp on this side of the river," she continued. "That trader over there with the big dog has just come in from the West. Somewhere out there he came across someone who spoke of Dr. Van Antwerp. We'll cross the river and find a campsite. Then I'll see what I can learn. They say the ferry is right down here at the end of Francis Street. Hurry along before the sun sets, Bert, or I'm not sure they'll take us on board."

The ferry was returning to the eastern bank as they drove down to the water's edge. Most of the emigrants were busy around supper fires, so the Van Antwerps had no trouble getting passage. The ferry was a small flatboat, propelled by two sweeps, enormous oars, each manned by one sweepman. The boat looked so small on the wide, eddying river that Charlotte after the first dizzy view closed her eyes tightly and gripped the edge of the seat. Each time she opened them a crack, dizziness threatened to upset her.

Charlotte heard a chuckle nearby. Carefully opening her eyes, she looked for the source of that chuckle. The Westerner who had ridden onto the ferry just ahead of them sat on his horse close to the front of the Van Antwerp wagon. Charlotte grinned at him and clutched the seat tighter.

"Just a wee mite dizzy?" he asked.

Charlotte nodded.

"Look way off to that line of hills in the west," he suggested kindly, "and you'll forget the current. Be thankful you're as late in the season as this. First wagon train I rode out with at the beginning of the season, the old Missouri was right wild."

Charlotte shivered and glanced at the swirling, muddy water.

The stranger chuckled again. After viewing their wagon and oxen he asked, "Come a far piece, have you?"

"Well . . ." Charlotte hesitated. She was not sure anymore what people called far. "From Wisconsin."

"Izzat so?" he asked, turning with interest. "Where 'bouts in Wisconsin? I've a letter given me by a feller in that first train I piloted, to be mailed to his family in Wisconsin . . . Oshkosh. Be you from anywhere's near to Oshkosh?"

Bert drew nearer and Mrs. Van Antwerp bent forward to hear the stranger more clearly. Charlotte wanted to look at the wagon to see if Oshkosh, Wisconsin, was painted on the tool chest or plow or the wooden frame. It was too much like a dream to have this total stranger speak so confidently of their tiny hometown off in Wisconsin.

"That's home!" Charlotte said, a bit breathlessly. "Oshkosh is where we come from!"

Mrs. Van Antwerp laughed shakily. "Are we awake— or are we dreaming? I—I'm Lottie Van Antwerp."

"Wal! I do—I do declare to goodness," the stranger said, as if his voice were used to much rougher exclamations. "Next time a body tells me you can't find a needle in a haystack, I'll say I done it onc't. Imagine, in all this caboodle of people, findin' the little Doc's family. I expected you

50

folks to be way back yonder in Wisconsin!"

Lottie Van Antwerp's voice still shook as she asked, "Have you really word from my husband, Dr. Van Antwerp, Dr. Johan Van Antwerp? How—how is he?"

"Chipper as a sparrow and busy as a bee."

Charlotte clapped her hands. It was indeed her own pa this tanned stranger was talking about, his description was so true.

"There's right much dysentery along the trail this spring," the man went on. "He hired out as a doctor for the first train that crossed the river, and bless you if he didn't nip those chills and runs so smartly that it's my guess his group will get through to Oregon healthiest of any of them."

"To Oregon?" Ma exclaimed. "Johan was bound for California."

"That he was," the stranger said. "And that's why I'm carrying this letter. Talking to this one and that one, your little Dr. Johan sort of got the idea that Oregon was a better place to settle his family than Californy. Then the Martin group came along needing a doctor, having lost their own to cholery not far back of St. Joe, and that changed the little Doc's mind for good. Well, well! So I don't have to mail this in St. Joe tomorrow after all."

He handed the letter to Mrs. Van Antwerp, who opened it, read, and wiped her eyes. Bert and Charlotte pressed against her, eager to read it, too.

"That's right!" she exclaimed. "Isn't that Johan for you? Decided that the Willamette Valley was better for us all than digging for gold with Waldo in California. More to my taste, too, I can tell you!"

"Oh, do let us hurry," cried Charlotte. "Maybe we can catch him."

51

"Not so fast, missy," the man said. "That Martin train is all of four weeks ahead of you."

The ferry grated against the western bank.

"But, at least," said Mrs. Van Antwerp as she climbed from the wagon to help Bert lead the oxen to shore, "we know we are headed in the right direction, rolling along in his very tracks."

As the wagon wheels crunched on the gravel road, Moses crawled out from the bedding and scrambled to the seat beside Charlotte. Before she could stop him, he leaped to the wagon tongue and ran along until he reached the lead team, Tim and Tuck. He jumped to Tuck's back and rode along tense and upright, his ears alert. Patient Tuck was unconcerned.

"Moses is the figurehead for our expedition," Charlotte said. "He'll bring us good luck because I think Good Luck is his middle name. He's odd-eyed and ever so many folks say odd-eyed cats are good luck. Already he's escaped drowning and escaped the storm. Now he'll be our figurehead, safe through to Calif—I mean—Oregon!"

Bert guided the oxen from the ferry to a little hollow not far from the road where their camp would be protected from the dust and crowds. Charlotte jumped from the

wagon and lifted Moses from Tuck's back. She sat down in the grass and watched Bert hastily build the supper fire.

"Did you ever see such golden sunshine?" she asked her mother as she squinted into the level rays of the setting sun. Her mother sank down to rest after the effort of helping Bert tether the oxen and Daisy.

"To be quite honest, Sharlie, I've never seen such golden sunlight myself. It's not often we get a letter that's like news from heaven." She patted the letter from Dr. Johan.

"Oh, I feel so close to Pa tonight," Charlotte said joyfully.

"Yes," said Ma as she jumped up, "and you'll get this close and no closer unless we make every minute count. You get supper, Charlotte, while Bert milks. I'm going to call on some of our neighbors. Who knows? Someone may need six helping hands to complete a train."

Charlotte watched anxiously as Moses ran up the bank after her mother. He had always come back from every expedition, but in this crowd of people and yipping dogs there were many places for a small black cat to get lost.

Mrs. Van Antwerp's face was sober when she returned in the dusk to eat her supper. Charlotte did not mention her anxiety about Moses.

"There's a group leaving in the morning," Ma reported. "But they aren't willing to take on a woman and two children. They say we aren't well-enough equipped. We haven't enough supplies, we ought to have another team of oxen, and our wagon doesn't look good for a long trip across prairie and desert and mountain."

Bert and Charlotte sat in shocked silence. Mrs. Van Antwerp finished her supper and rose to help Charlotte wash dishes and put camp in order for the night.

"Don't look so glum," Ma said. "Tomorrow I'm going back across the river to add to our food supply. No more oxen, though. I can't afford it. I trust this old wagon to hold together, but we certainly don't want to be beholden to our neighbors for food."

Charlotte mixed a gruel of milk and corn bread and a smidgen of the salt codfish from breakfast she had saved all day for Moses. She hoped the sound of the spoon against his saucer would lure him in from the dark. She set the saucer on the chest with the thud that always brought Moses scampering. But when she jumped over the wheel to the grass, there was no cat anywhere. She climbed to the level of the road and walked slowly up and down. There was no cat in sight. Softly she called, "Moses? Moses? Here kitty!"

At last her mother called impatiently, "Charlotte, we can't sit up all night for that cat!"

Bert was in his bedroll at the front of the wagon. Charlotte crawled quietly under her blanket. Long after her mother was asleep Charlotte lay awake. She listened for Moses until at last she fell asleep. Many times she wakened, lonesome for her pet.

The next day Ma crossed the river to St. Joseph to talk with other groups of emigrants and to buy supplies. Shortly after noon she came for Bert to hitch up Nip and Sam to the wagon to pick up her purchases.

"You stay close to camp and watch the livestock, Charlotte," Ma directed. "I've been told there's much thieving and we can't stand any more losses."

When she started the supper fire, Charlotte decided she'd boil the eggs. Cooking the same things in a different way might help their spirits. She'd make biscuits, too, instead of johnnycake.

With supper begun, Charlotte pulled grass to push through the slats of the chicken crate. She made many trips up the slope to watch for Ma and Bert and Moses. How she wished Moses would come bounding toward her!

When she finally saw Bert and Ma and the team approaching from the ferry, she hurried to pull the Dutch oven away from the heat. Her biscuits were never as fluffy and light as Ma's, and overbaking would make them even worse.

Sitting beside the fire was Moses, a battered and sorry-looking cat, but Moses just the same. His blue eye was swollen shut again; his left ear stood out on its side. With all that, he lifted his face and rubbed against Charlotte's legs, purring.

Charlotte hugged him. "You naughty kitty! You've been fighting again! What shall I ever do with you?"

Hurriedly she gave Moses a saucer of milk to keep him from underfoot while she buttered biscuits, peeled hard-boiled eggs, poured coffee for her mother and milk for Bert and herself.

When they had eaten, they stowed away the purchases of meal and flour, more of the endless salt pork, and a bag of dried fruit. Mrs. Van Antwerp had bought a cast-iron camp stove and a small tent, too.

"We'll be happier trailmates," she explained, "if we're not disturbing each other all night long."

Setting up the tent was a lark. It was to be Bert's, but Charlotte with Moses cuddled in her arms tried it out. However, playing at camping could not be fun for long with the sobering knowledge that no train captain wanted to add the Van Antwerps to his group.

6 Three days passed, with several wagon trains setting out for the West each day. New groups came in from the East. Ma went from group to group trying to find a place for the Van Antwerps to travel to Oregon.

"Why should they act so about us?" Charlotte asked. "I think they're hateful."

"No," Mrs. Antwerp corrected her, "they're frightened, just scared that we'll be a drag and hold them back. Anyone starting this late has a race with winter. Somehow we've got to find a way to be so useful that they'll be glad to invite us to join them."

But how? Charlotte wondered glumly.

For two days Moses stayed close to camp, nursing his wounds and babying his stiffness. But late on the third afternoon he started nosing through the grass, climbing farther from the fire. He pounced on a field mouse, and after eating it he climbed to the top of the rise. Charlotte followed him. Suddenly a mangy brown-and-white dog sighted Moses and, ki-yiing shrilly, started after the cat.

Moses flattened himself close to the ground and streaked off through the camps, darting under wagons, around camp-fires, behind tents, with the dog barking after him. Charlotte held her skirts high and chased the dog.

Behind the last camp was a row of trees—safety to Moses. He streaked through the camp, narrowly avoiding a tall boy with a load of wood. Just as the dog reached him Moses scurried up a tree.

Charlotte stopped, breathless. The boy had dropped his armload of wood in surprise as the cat and dog dashed past him. Now he stood grinning at Charlotte.

"I'm Charlotte Van Antwerp," she said. "I'm sorry that Moses upset your camp. It's that dog's fault."

"Pleased to meet you," the boy said. "I'm Reuben Warren. That dog has been a pest all week. No need for you to be apologizing because of him. Get out of here, you cur!" he said, running at the dog.

The animal went off yelping toward the river. Charlotte and Reuben laughed as they watched its cowardly retreat.

"He belonged to the fellow my pa hired to help herd the cattle in our train across to Oregon. Pa's captain of this train," Reuben explained proudly, indicating the circle of wagons nearby. "And then this fellow's sister backed out. My pa had hired her to be the schoolmarm for my sisters, but when she saw a crowd of Indians—Pa said they were Pottawattomies and friendly as could be—she got scared and started back home. Her brother went along. That's why we're still here. Pa needs a herder, and he promised Ma we'd not roll one wagon-length toward Oregon without a teacher."

Charlotte said quickly, "My ma's a teacher, and she wants to go to Oregon in the worst kind of way—and my brother Bert is the best in the world with animals."

"You don't say!" Reuben exclaimed. He grabbed Charlotte by the arm and led her toward the campfire.

A tall man rose from the wagon and looked curiously at Charlotte as Reuben said, "Pa, I've found us a teacher!"

"Oh, sir, I'm not the teacher. It's my mother," Charlotte

told him. "She was a schoolteacher back East before Pa married her and brought her to Wisconsin. She teaches my brothers and me every day we aren't working on the farm. She has been trying for days to find a wagon train that we can join."

A woman in a rocking chair before the campfire stood up, clasping her hands. "Oh, Edgar, let's hire her."

Charlotte looked at the woman with interest. She seemed as out of place in an emigrant camp as her cherrywood rocker looked beside a stained covered wagon on the prairie. She was tiny and elaborately dressed in a gown of sprigged dimity.

"As soon as I get my cat out of that tree," Charlotte said, "I'll take you to my mother. We're camped in that little hollow over near the ferry. Ma's name is Mrs. Johan Van Antwerp."

"I suppose Reuben can help you get your cat," Mrs. Warren said. "But don't leave your sisters unprotected, son, and keep that cat away from here. Come, Edgar, let's hire this teacher before another train that wants to hang on to civilization even in this wilderness finds her."

Charlotte watched as the little woman hurried across the rough ground toward the river. Reuben's tall father followed meekly. He might be the captain of the wagon train, but tiny Mrs. Warren seemed to be the commander of the captain!

"Your mother is pretty," Charlotte told Reuben softly.

"Nobody else like her," Reuben said proudly. "Come on. Let's get your cat."

Three heads appeared then at the opening of the Warrens' covered wagon. They belonged to three black-haired girls, large, medium, and tiny.

"Cat? Where's the cat?" asked the tiny girl.

"Charlotte's cat, up a tree, Alice, honey," Reuben told her. "You girls be good while I help."

Alice held out her arms to Reuben. He lifted her and swung her to the ground. Then he gave a hand to the next sister. "Charlotte, this is Sophronia, but she's Phronny for everyday. And this is Lucy. They're the ones your ma is supposed to teach."

"Where's the kitty? Where's the kitty?" Alice demanded.

Charlotte turned and ran to the tree. The Warren children followed.

Moses was hunched far out on a limb. When he saw Charlotte he stood up, his fur on end, his tail a quivering plume. Charlotte held her arms up to him, but he crouched on the branch and yowled.

"That won't help," Reuben said. "Don't you know that cats are good go-uppers and no good at all as come-downers? Here, get out of my way."

Reuben started hitching himself up the tree trunk. As he climbed to the branch where the cat stood, Moses arched his back, lashed his tail and hissed, then clawed higher.

Reuben dropped to the ground. "Wow, that's a real wildcat you have," he said.

"Poor kitty, poor kitty," Alice called, holding her arms up.

"Well, what do we do now?" Reuben asked, rubbing his hands where Moses had struck him.

"Mamma's really going to be cross about that scratch," Lucy warned.

"Mamma doesn't like cats," Reuben admitted. "You'll have to keep him out of her sight. But what are we going to do now?"

Charlotte looked over her shoulder to make sure no one was watching. "Nothing for me to do but climb. Maybe I'll only have to go as far as that first branch. You'll have to be real quiet now."

"Ladies don't climb trees," Lucy said primly.

"Aw, be still, Lucy," Reuben commanded.

Charlotte circled the rough trunk of the tree with her arms and started to hitch herself upward.

"She's as good a climber as you are, Reuben," Phonny said admiringly.

Little Alice clapped her hands and called, "Goody! Get the kitty!"

Charlotte sat on the first branch catching her breath and blowing on her hands. They stung and burned from pulling herself up the tree. Moses, alarmed by the movement and suspicious even of Charlotte, backed along the branch on which he had been crouching.

Charlotte began to talk softly without making any movement to startle him. The Warren children remained quiet. At last Moses crouched down, his fur flattened, and his tail returned to normal. Charlotte waited patiently.

Slowly she rose to a standing position, but the branch dipped under her weight and she had to steady herself. Moses hissed and backed toward the trunk again.

Charlotte was absolutely motionless and coaxed, "Moses, don't be scared. See, it's Sharlie."

Lucy sniffed, "You don't talk to cats like you do to people."

"Be still! You'll scare him further up that tree," Reuben warned.

Moses kept his back to the trunk but he settled down and blinked at Charlotte. Talking softly, she inched along her branch until she was immediately beneath him, her hand only inches away. Moses reached out and licked one of her fingers.

Alice and Phronny gasped and Moses drew back. Charlotte kept up her sing-song begging and did not move. Then Moses at last crept along her arm to her shoulder and nestled his head under her chin. Clasping him, Charlotte sat down on the limb.

"Now I'm afraid to jump," she admitted. She looked out toward the river just then and saw Bert guiding the family wagon toward the Warren train. The two women on the seat were her mother and Mrs. Warren. Captain Warren rode beside them.

Charlotte felt frozen and unable to move. Bert halted the wagon and Captain Warren looked at her and frowned. "What is the meaning of this?" he asked.

The explanations did not satisfy him. "A girl climbing a tree!" he said with disapproval.

"And because of a cat," Mrs. Warren said with distaste. "Mrs. Van Antwerp, do you really intend to let your daughter take that animal all the way to Oregon?"

Ma looked up at Charlotte. "That cat saved Charlotte from a cyclone, Mrs. Warren. We feel as if he's earned his right to be a member of the family. I don't think any of us wants to leave him behind."

"Hmm!" grunted Captain Warren. "You would feel attached to him after that, I suppose. As long as you keep him from causing any disturbance you may take him."

A troubled look crossed Ma's face, but before she could answer, Mrs. Warren touched her arm. "My girls have been brought up to be ladies, Mrs. Van Antwerp. I do hope you'll labor extra hard to see that they get none of your daughter's tree-climbing habits."

Mrs. Van Antwerp bowed politely, but her mouth was a thin line before she spoke. "My daughter, too, is brought up to be a lady, Mrs. Warren. Such things as tree climbing happen only when some creature is in need of help."

"Enough of this," said Captain Warren abruptly. He stepped beneath the tree, held up this arms, and Charlotte slipped into them and then down onto the ground.

"Now let us be about our evening chores," the captain said. "Our party is complete with herder and teacher. We'll take to the trail at sunup."

"Goody! Goody!" little Alice sang. "Wheels are going round and round again—off to Oregon, and Sharlie, and Moses-kitty are going, too!"

Night should be for sleeping, Charlotte thought, but she lay awake for a long time. The Van Antwerps' wagon had been drawn up next to the Warrens', in the very center of the encampment.

The camp was like a little village Charlotte realized as she listened to the night noises. The people of the train had elected Reuben's father to be their captain, just as the people in a village elected a mayor. Old Mr. Smithers, whom the Van Antwerps had met at suppertime, was the pilot who would guide the way. He would be like a village constable or policeman. Most of his life he had hunted and trapped on the prairies, deserts, and mountains beyond the Mississippi. His knowledge would serve the emigrants well.

Charlotte decided that she felt safe in this train with Captain Warren as a strict leader and Mr. Smithers as an experienced guide. But still she could not sleep, and Moses, tired of her restlessness, jumped out of the wagon. When a shot from the night watchman's rifle roused the camp at dawn Charlotte felt as if she'd just closed her eyes.

A quick breakfast over a tiny fire was enough for the Van Antwerps. As newcomers in the train they did not want to keep anyone waiting. Bert milked Daisy while Charlotte helped Ma pack the wagon. They were ready when Reuben and Captain Warren came for Bert. He was to ride horseback with Reuben and the other big boys and unmarried

64

men to herd the cattle at the end of the train. Ma would drive the team of oxen.

Captain Warren explained, "I'd like to have you follow right along behind our wagon. Then, when time comes for nooning, you and Mrs. Warren can make plans for the schooling."

Charlotte did not care what place her family had in the wagon train. All that mattered was that the bustle of camp and the smells of breakfast had failed to bring Moses back from his night's wandering. She was taken by surprise when two freckle-faced, silver-haired little girls climbed into the wagon next to hers and stuck out their tongues.

"Stuck up! Stuck up!" called the larger girl. "Last come, first placed. 'Tain't fair!"

The pilot's bugle sounded for the start, and Moses darted out of the tall grass. Charlotte jumped over the wheel, gathered up her cat, and threw herself into the back of the wagon just as her mother maneuvered Tim and Tuck, Nip and Sam into the trail after the Warren wagon.

One of the towheaded girls on the seat of the wagon behind stuck out her tongue again. With her thumbs in her ears she waved her hands like big donkey ears at Charlotte. Her mother glowered.

Tears smarted in Charlotte's eyes. Was this how traveling on the trail was going to be? Mrs. Van Antwerp turned and saw what was happening. "Don't cry over someone making faces," she said. "Remember, people are scared of this long trip and sad about leaving their homes. When someone's scared and sad, being first in line may mean a lot."

"But we didn't ask for this place," Charlotte objected.

"Scared, sad people don't think clearly," Ma answered.

"Maybe things can be straightened out at nooning. We'll try to be friendly to those little girls. We'll need each other many times before this trip is over."

As they jolted along they passed other groups still eating their breakfast or hurrying to pack their wagons.

"It's good to get an early start," Ma said. "We're lucky we found a place with a hustler like Captain Warren."

"But he never smiles," Charlotte said. "He makes me feel afraid."

"Nothing to be afraid about if you behave yourself," her mother said, looking at Charlotte with one eyebrow lifted. "It's a big responsibility to be a leader of a group of people starting along this dangerous trail. He has his own family worries, too, like the rest of us," she added after a moment. "I took it from their talk last night that Mrs. Warren didn't want to leave their home back east. She's delicate, and he thinks the mild winters in the Willamette Valley will be good for her."

"Like for Pa," Charlotte said.

"That's right," said Ma. "It seems as if a lot of folk set off for the same reason. And it doesn't make Captain Warren's worries any easier that before we cross the mountains, Mrs. Warren will be having their new baby."

"Oh, my goodness!" exclaimed Charlotte.

"So see to it that you don't get into any escapades to annoy the captain."

"I promise," said Charlotte earnestly.

Hour after hour, the wagons jolted along the deeply rutted trail worn in the grassy plain by hundreds of wheels that had gone before them on the Oregon Trail.

Their train made a wide curve, skirting a marshland. By hanging on the frame of the wagon and leaning out Charlotte could count fourteen wagons followed closely by the boys with the cattle and extra horses. Not far behind them came the first wagon of another group.

A short distance ahead of Captain Warren's big prairie schooner was another line of travelers. An almost unbroken train of wagons stretched across the prairie as far as Charlotte could see.

As the sun climbed higher and the grass dried, the girls in the wagon behind the Van Antwerps jumped out to play along the trail and pick flowers. Other children joined them. One boy had an old string ball, and soon the children were in a lively game of toss and catch.

Charlotte remained knitting on the seat beside Ma. Her body ached from jolting along the rough trail in the springless wagon. She loved a game of catch, but she felt the children would not welcome her.

When they reached a clump of trees on the bank of a brook, the pilot stopped them for nooning. The shade of the trees and the cool running water were a joy after the morning on the hot, dusty trail.

Charlotte took a long time to unhitch the oxen. They could browse without being yoked. She stroked gentle Sam's nose. She patted Tim. She scratched Tuck between the horns, and she gingerly offered spunky Nip a handful of grass.

Ma lit a fire and scrambled the eggs she had taken from the chicken crate. Bert trotted up on the swaybacked old horse Captain Warren had furnished him. He took a tin plate of cold biscuit and scrambled eggs and attacked it with a huge appetite. He was jaunty and excited. His pleasure in the company of the boys showed Charlotte how much he missed Johnny. Charlotte poured a saucer of milk for Moses, then she sat down to eat beside Bert.

Men were talking loudly and angrily around Captain Warren's wagon. Soon the entire group, led by Captain Warren, came toward the Van Antwerp wagon. The captain looked stiff and uncomfortable.

He cleared his throat and glanced from his wife to the angry men. "Mrs. Van Antwerp, these men feel that I'm being unfair. They think last to join the train should be at the end of the line. But my wife is worried that you'll not be able to tend to your teaching from way back there at the end of the line."

"Last come, last served does seem fairest, doesn't it?"

68

Mrs. Van Antwerp said pleasantly. "Don't worry, Mrs. Warren. Nights and nooning I'll be teaching, and we'll all be together in circle anyway. I think I'd like to be at the end of the line—gives me a better chance to keep an eye on my little milk cow and my big boy."

Everyone laughed and relaxed. Charlotte thought Ma did not need to envy Pa's diplomacy. She had enough of her own, and to spare. Captain and Mrs. Warren shook hands with Mrs. Van Antwerp.

"Just as soon as supper is over," Ma said, "I'll sit down with your girls and Charlotte, and-I'll let them each read a bit, so I can decide where to place them."

When the teams were hitched to the wagons and the train started off across the prairie, the Van Antwerps waited until fifteen wagons had passed. As the unfriendly tow-headed girls rode by, Charlotte suddenly grinned widely and felt tempted to make big, slow donkey ears at them.

As the warm afternoon stretched on, Charlotte tired of the jolting wagon. They came upon Phronny Warren waiting at the side of the trail. "Pa said I could come back and walk with you," she said. "Come on down."

To run no risk of being caught by the great wheel, Charlotte crawled through the wagon and dropped to the ground at the back.

"All those Turner girls do is quarrel and say bad words, so Ma won't let me play with them anymore," Phronny said.

For the rest of the afternoon Charlotte and Phronny walked along the slow-moving train, picking flowers and scaring garter snakes. Charlotte was weary when the call was sounded to make camp for the night, but she had learned much from Phronny about the families in the wagon train.

At the direction of Captain Warren and Mr. Smithers, the wagons formed a large circle. The tongue of one wagon was chained to the rear axle of the next. The cast-iron stoves were set up in the center of the circle.

While Bert milked Daisy, Charlotte filled their stove with dry twigs she had gathered as she walked with Phronny. Last of all she tucked in a twist of paper. She stepped back to watch as Ma opened her tinderbox. There was a special skill to lighting a fire with flint and steel. Ma guarded the tiny spark from the brisk breeze. She blew gently until the fire was a steady, spreading flame.

When the potatoes and the hamhocks were boiling, Mrs. Van Antwerp handed Charlotte a pail, saying "Fetch and set to boil a kettle of water to give us safe drinking water. This will be your duty, Charlotte, and see that you don't fail. Remember, your father always said that in a new country the best way to stay well is to have good water."

With that task done, Charlotte looked around the camp circle. Before every wagon but one a column of smoke rose into the evening air and pots boiled. Mrs. Turner knelt before her stove, striking her flint with nervous movements that brought no welcome spark. A baby screamed in the big girl's arms. Mr. Turner was nowhere in sight.

"Look, Ma," exclaimed Charlotte. "She can't get her fire started. Should I take our shovel and carry some embers to her?"

"I think that's a first-rate idea," said Ma. "Here, take a twist of paper to make sure it gets a start."

Scooping the pile of embers from the little stove, Charlotte took the twist of paper and ran across the camp.

"Here, ma'am, start your fire with this," Charlotte said, "and save your tinderbox."

She dumped the embers into the little stove and stuck the twist of paper into the center. In a moment the Turners' wood had caught fire and a sixteenth spiral of smoke rose.

"Why—why—" sputtered Mrs. Turner. "I'm much obleeged to you. . . ."

"Oh, that's all right," Charlotte stammered. Turning quickly, she ran back.

After supper, Captain Warren set out a heavy box of books. Mrs. Van Antwerp had Phronny and Lucy and Charlotte read for her until she determined which reader each child should use. Then, while the three girls sat cross-legged around the campfire and read silently, Mrs. Van Antwerp took Alice on her lap and guided her finger around the shape of each letter in the alphabet. Mrs. Warren sat in her rocker at the edge of the group, fanning herself to drive away mosquitoes. She smiled happily to see her children studying again.

"No one ever had such a queer schoolroom," Phronny whispered to Charlotte. "No roof, no floor, no walls!" Marking her place on the page with one finger, Charlotte whispered, "Best of all, no boys!"

When it was too dark to read, Captain Warren packed the books away before dew could damage them. As the smaller children were called to bed a fiddle tuned up across the circle. Older boys and girls sang and danced for a little while, but as the stars grew bright, the travelers, tired from their first day of real Oregon Trail journeying, went one by one to sleep.

Day by day the wagon train moved slowly northwestward across the prairie. Each new day was patterned after the last one: rifle shots to waken everyone before dawn; the commanding voice of the bugle to set them on their way. A stream to be crossed added uncertainty for the men and variety for the children. Brooks were a break in the monotony and a freshener after the dusty air. Large creeks and rivers with unknown dangers quickened the heartbeat of everyone.

Shortly after noon one hot June day, ten days out from St. Joseph, the emigrants were about to cross the border into Nebraska. They halted at a sizable creek with high banks. Soon Charlotte heard men's voices rumbling in the heat.

"Run ahead and see what's happened," Mrs. Van Antwerp said as she swung around to prop her feet on the seat.

Charlotte jumped to the ground. She hesitated uneasily when Moses leaped down and gamboled after her, but she decided that he would follow her back.

When she reached the Warren wagon, Phronny beckoned from the pucker-hole at the back.

"Does your ma know you're out?" Phronny asked breathlessly. "Our ma pushed us into the wagon so we'll not see them."

"See what?" Charlotte asked. "Mamma sent me to find out why we're stopped."

"It's the bridge across the creek," Lucy explained. "Indians built it, and my father and Mr. Smithers are bargaining about toll. You'd better run right back to your wagon because those Indians are just about bare naked."

Just then Charlotte heard Moses hissing on the other side of the wagon. She ran forward in time to see a tall Indian wearing only a breechcloth and a battered straw hat drop Moses and shake his hand, blowing on deep scratches. Moses ran to the safety of Charlotte's arms.

Charlotte looked up to see herself the center of attention. The Indians were tall, broad-shouldered, some of them wearing trousers, others, like the man who had been scratched by Moses, dressed only in breechcloths.

Captain Warren glowered at Charlotte for creating a delay, but Mr. Smithers gave her one of his quick smiles.

The Indian with the scratched hand spoke rapidly to Mr. Smithers, who listened carefully and then turned to Charlotte.

"He's taken a fancy to yer kitty, Miss Charlotte," the pilot translated. "Says he'll let yer ma's wagon cross the bridge free of the twenty-five cents for toll if you give it to him. Says there must be powerful magic in a beast with odd eyes like that. What d'ye say? Is it a bargain?"

"Give up Moses?" Charlotte exclaimed. "Oh, no!"

The Indians gathered closer to the girl. The man Moses had scratched sensed her refusal before Mr. Smithers could speak. He scowled.

"Do you mean to say," Captain Warren asked sharply, "that you'd put us in bad with the Indians just to hold on to a useless pet?"

73

Feeling that the others agreed with Captain Warren that she was being selfish, she could not answer. She hugged Moses and looked at her dusty shoes, wishing she had made Moses stay in the wagon.

When the silence was almost too much to bear Charlotte felt a hand on her shoulder and her mother asked, "What is the trouble here?"

Everyone except Charlotte began to speak at once. When she had sorted out the crisis from the babble of words Mrs. Van Antwerp smiled and went to the Indian who had been scratched. She shook his hand and then turned to Mr. Smithers.

"Tell him this cat doesn't trust men," she said. "Tell him that yowls and scratches are probably all he'd get. Tell him that if he'll let my daughter keep her cat I'll not only pay my toll but give him this gold chain and locket."

Charlotte gasped. Her mother was giving away the gold chain and locket her own father had given her for passing her state examinations with high grades when she graduated from the district school back in New York. Charlotte stepped to her mother's side, choking with distress. But Mrs. Van Antwerp, shaking her head slightly, put her arm around Charlotte and waited while Mr. Smithers talked with the Indian.

"Says he'd be pleased with such a deal," Mr. Smithers said finally.

Mrs. Van Antwerp gave the Indian her chain and locket and twenty-five cents from the purse fastened to her belt. The bargaining with the bridge owners had been completed, and as Charlotte and her mother walked arm-in-arm back to their place, the Warren wagon clattered across the bridge.

After pouring milk into the saucer to hold Moses' interest until the wagon was in motion, Charlotte crawled back to the seat beside her mother.

"You shouldn't have done it, Mamma!" Charlotte said, sniffing back tears. "That's the only keepsake you had left after the cyclone—and Grandpa gave it to you so long ago, and—"

"And—and—and—" said Mrs. Van Antwerp, laying her finger across Charlotte's lips. "You wouldn't want to leave our kitty in an Indian village. And we wouldn't want to cause still more bad feelings between the Indians and the white men. He's happy, that young Sac Indian, and I'm happy that I had something to make him happy. Here comes Mr. Smithers to tell me to keep these wheels rolling!"

It was a rude log bridge and it seemed rickety, perched high on the banks of the swift creek. Each loaded wagon passed safely across, however. The flooring of the bridge was nothing but poles laid across the logs, jolting passengers in the wagons as much as did the ruts of the trail.

As June circled on toward month's end, the wagons toiled onward, twenty miles on a good day, ten on a bad day— onward, onward, onward to the Platte River. The heat grew worse. The sun beat down mercilessly, and Charlotte no longer had to be reminded to keep her sunbonnet on. Moses slept through the long days in his special place under the wagon seat.

Every day was the same as the one before it. Always ahead of the Van Antwerps was the Hood wagon, bulging with little Hoods. It moved briskly along, pulled by three teams of horses. Ahead of the Hoods were the other wagons of the Warren group, and never out of sight were the wagons of another party. Behind the Van Antwerps came the animals belonging to the Warren train. Always they moved over what seemed to be the same deep ruts worn in the same unending grassy prairie.

Lesson time in the evenings gave variety to their days. First there was reading and a bit of spelling. Then came brain-stretching sums and subtractions that Mrs. Van Antwerp expected her pupils to give at the snap of her finger. Finally as darkness fell books were put away. The teacher cuddled Alice on her lap and talked to the children about the Oregon country.

"How do you know so much about it?" Lucy Warren asked suspiciously one evening. "You haven't been there anymore than we have!"

Slowly Mrs. Van Antwerp undressed Alice, who had fallen asleep. Mrs. Warren brought a nightgown from the wagon, and Alice was tucked into the trundle bed without being wakened.

"No, you're right, Lucy," Mrs. Van Antwerp said after Alice was gone. "I've never been to Oregon. But my husband, Dr. Van Antwerp, always wanted to go west. Night after night while I darned his stockings he read everything he could find about California and the Oregon country. It's surprising how much you can learn that way."

Lucy nodded at that, and the next day she tried her knowledge of the Oregon country with other travelers. And so every night a few more children joined the lesson circle.

One evening Mrs. Antwerp encouraged the children to talk about their home states. The Warrens and Browns came from Pennsylvania. The Sawyers came from Maine, and the Aldens from Massachusetts. New York was home for the Hoods, and the Baxters claimed Ohio. The Turners were from Kentucky and the Harrises from Tennessee.

Spelling matches attracted some of the older children and soon the twenty-four girls and boys of school age met almost every evening.

The Turners held out the longest against lesson times. "Uppity folks wastin' hardworking folkses' time with books," Mrs. Turner complained.

One night there was gingerbread for supper. Mrs. Van Antwerp had baked it, using the Dutch oven and keeping the fire up while they ate their meat and potatoes. At the end of the humdrum trail meal gingerbread was a real treat.

After supper Ma put the leftover gingerbread into the little tin lunch pail. "Take this to Bert," she told Charlotte. "Tell him to divide it with all his friends."

With Moses at her heels, Charlotte slipped through the barricade of linked wagons and skipped across the grass to the herdsmen guarding the cattle for the night. They sat around a little fire listening to the eldest Turner boy, Danny, strum a battered banjo as he sang "Oh! Susanna, Don't You Cry for Me."

When he had finished that he sang, "Listen to the Mocking Bird," and then "Hush, Li'l Baby, Don't You Cry."

"That's good," exclaimed Charlotte admiringly when Dan stopped. "Do you know some others?"

"Oh, sure," said Dan. "My ma used to be always singing to us. But that was before Pa decided to go to Oregon. Ma'd rather stayed back home in Kentucky."

Charlotte gave Bert the gingerbread and ran to tell Ma about Dan's music.

That night when the girls were busy working multiplication problems on the fire shovel with pieces of coal for pencils, Mrs. Van Antwerp went to the herders' fire. As darkness fell and Captain Warren was packing the books, she brought Dan into the circle. "Dan doesn't have to guard until midnight," she explained, "so he is going to sing and play for us."

Everyone enjoyed the singing time, and in the flickering firelight no one was too shy to join. As Charlotte and Phronny swayed together to the music, arm-in-arm, they noticed the older Turner girls standing on the edge of the circle.

The next night Dan came to the Warren fire at lesson time, with his sisters timidly following.

"If it is going to be one of your geography lessons, I'd be pleased to be learning something about the Oregon country," he said. "And Essie and Lettie would like some book learning, too."

Nodding happily, Mrs. Van Antwerp set Essie to read with Lucy. Mattie shared a book with Charlotte, and Phronny and Lettie used the same reader.

The next night the three-year-old Turner, Midge, came tagging along with the older girls. Mrs. Van Antwerp took both Midge and Alice Warren on her lap and taught them letters together. When Peter-Paul, the Turner baby, finally fell asleep, Mrs. Turner, tired from the long day with the fretful baby, fell asleep beside him.

Dan came at the end of almost every lesson time with his banjo. It was good to sing together to help keep spirits up, for there were many sad nights along the trail. Cholera had spread rapidly. Several times each day the travelers passed graves, bare and lonely.

Charlotte hugged Moses closely and said, "Oh, I do hope Pa is safe and well."

One warm evening Mr. Smithers guided them into a

camp circle within sight of a little fort named Kearney. "Built three-four years back," Mr. Smithers told the children, to protect travelers from the Indians.

Outside the quadrangle of the log military buildings were a few other buildings. There was a boardinghouse "run by the Mormons," Mr. Smithers explained, so the children looked at it with curiosity. There was also a stage station with a stable to house the changes of horses needed by fast-traveling mail coaches.

Away so long from settled life, Charlotte stared at the fort with interest. This soon turned to concern when she saw a yellow tabby cat sunning on the boardinghouse steps. She was debating whether to confine Moses to the wagon when Phronny ran up waving a piece of paper.

"I'm going to write a letter to my grandpa. Why don't you, too?" she panted. "That little sod house is the post office, and we can mail our letters by stagecoach. It comes through day after tomorrow. Can't mail letters again for sure until we get to Fort Laramie."

As Phronny ran off, Charlotte got paper from her mother, who with a faraway look on her face was writing to Grandma and Grandpa Bertrand, way back in New York State.

"May I send my letter to Mrs. Pennywell and tell her Moses is a good traveler?" Charlotte asked.

The letter was just finished when Phronny came bouncing back. Ma showed Charlotte how to tuck one folded side of the letter inside a second fold. After addressing the folded letter to Mrs. Pennywell, Oshkosh, Wisconsin, Charlotte took the two letters and the coins her mother gave her, twenty-five cents for each letter.

There was much to see on the way to mail the letters:

Pawnee Indians camped outside the log walls of the fort, soldiers gathered around the flagpole, the stableman and his wife, the postmaster.

Charlotte did not notice that Moses had followed until he suddenly stalked ahead, stiff legged, hair bristling, and eyes gleaming an angry red. Too late she saw the tabby cat from the boardinghouse jump from the top step yowling a challenge.

Charlotte darted toward Moses, but her hands closed on empty air. The two cats were a black and yellow blur, rolling over and over. They separated long enough for the tabby to shake himself free and dash across the yard to the stable. Moses raced after him, and the cats disappeared into the dark interior. The girls dared not follow.

"Oh!" wailed Charlotte. "That big old cat will kill Moses for sure!"

Phronny was not sympathetic. "Come on, Sharlie, we have to mail our letters," she urged.

When the girls came out into the orange light of the setting sun all was quiet in the stable and there was no sign of either cat.

Charlotte dawdled as much as she could, but Phronny insisted, "Hurry up! We want to finish supper so we can watch the soldiers lower the flag."

All through supper Charlotte watched for Moses, but he did not appear. Still hoping he would come, she helped tidy the camp for night.

Only when her mother finished and strolled slowly toward the parade ground in the center of the fort did Charlotte join the other girls. While they listened to the bugle and fife and drums and watched the soldiers maneuver, Charlotte's eyes searched for one black cat. All she saw was the yellow tabby, more than a little battle scarred, washing himself.

"If Moses would only come," she said to her mother back at camp.

"Stop worrying," Ma answered. "Cats usually take care of themselves. Tomorrow's the Fourth of July and Captain Warren says we'll stay to watch the soldiers parade and listen to the Commandant read the Declaration of Independence. Moses will be back by then. Now go to bed."

The Fourth of July was bright and warm. Everyone was in a festive mood—everyone but Charlotte and Mr. Smithers, who was sharing Van Antwerp food this week.

" 'Tain't good!" he said dolefully as he gulped his last cup of coffee and prepared to go to the fort. "To be sure of a safe trip clear to the Willamette Valley a group oughter be at Independence Rock on Independence Day."

The clear, piercing notes of the Army bugle summoned them all to the fort. As Charlotte walked beside her mother, she noticed the worry unmasked momentarily on her mother's face at Mr. Smithers' mention of their poor progress on the trail. With the anxiety of a train starting out too late in the season, she knew she should not be moping about her cat. But her gloom deepened when she saw the yellow tabby limping across the stable yard and no sign of Moses.

In spite of herself, Charlotte was stirred at the brave sound of the soldiers' bugles, at the snap of the flag as it unfurled at the top of the flagpole, and at the moving words of the Declaration of Independence. At the end, Mr. Alden, the preacher with the Warren group, said a prayer. Then the travelers went quietly to drive their wagons into the line of daily march.

Charlotte's heart ached. She dared not expect this train, already a month late, to delay its progress because one small black cat was missing.

The soldiers at the fort fired a salute and the bugles sounded as the first wagon in line moved creakingly westward. A small dark shadow shot out of the stable doorway and streaked across the open space to the Van Antwerp wagon.

With a happy cry Charlotte leaped down, gathered up Moses, and was back on the wagon seat just as it was time to move.

Moses had a fresh gash on his ear, but he gave a jaunty toss with his sleek black head and settled down on Charlotte's lap.

One hot Saturday afternoon Charlotte stared ahead in surprise. The Hoods' wagon had suddenly disappeared!

Charlotte shut her eyes and rubbed them before reopening them again. Hoods' wagon *was* gone. Now Tim and Tuck, Nip and Sam were straining against their yokes, pulling the Van Antwerp wagon to the crest of a little hill —a hill when there had been for days and days only monotonous, level prairie. Now the Hood wagon reappeared ahead, and the loose animals and their herders were suddenly hidden from Charlotte's sight.

Ma straightened up, startled, for she had been napping on the seat.

"Look, Ma, look!" shrieked Charlotte. "It's a hill! The flatness is gone. I can measure that we're really moving at last."

Charlotte crawled through the wagon and jumped down. Now the cattle and spare horses appeared at the crest of the little hill, ready to follow the wagons down into a shallow valley.

Phronny Warren ran back along the length of the train toward Charlotte. "Race you to the top of the next hill!" she challenged. "Maybe we can see the Rocky Mountains."

There were no mountains in sight at the hillcrest, only another grassy valley with a creek running through it. Beyond was prairie and then more gentle hills, like the one they had just climbed. Hill after hill, they sloped away into the blue distance.

"Oh, dear!" sighed Phronny. "It's too hot to run, and there are no mountains after all."

"Ma told us last night that we have to get beyond the Platte River before we see any real mountains. Remember?" Charlotte asked. "But, look, your father and Mr. Smithers are circling the wagons by the creek. I wonder why. It's a long time before sunset."

Soon the girls saw Lucy coming toward them. "We're stopping so everybody can wash clothes. Phronny, you have to help carry water. And Charlotte, you'd better not let Moses come nosing around our camp. Mamma doesn't like him. She hasn't forgotten how he almost got us into trouble scratching that Indian. I hate to tell you, but Papa says if Moses ever bothers Mamma he'll give him a bullet where it will do the most good."

Charlotte stopped, aghast at Lucy's warning. She ran back to where her mother was maneuvering the wagon into the circle. She was tempted to share her problem with Ma, but she hesitated. Ma had worries enough.

Bert rode up to help pitch camp and carry water. Mrs. Van Antwerp started the fire.

"Fill all the kettles with water," she directed. "I feel— and you both look—as if I've not done washing since Methuselah was a boy!"

It was good to hear Ma joking. The creek was beautiful with a clear deep pool, and below it, ripples chuckled over stones. But Charlotte was worried about Moses. Phronny joined her as she dipped her last pail of water.

"I'm sorry, Sharlie," she said softly, looking over her

84

shoulder to make sure Lucy was out of earshot. "Alice and Reuben and I like Moses. But Lucy's funny like Mamma—she's afraid of cats. And Papa does everything that Mamma says. He really did say that about giving Moses a bullet."

"But cats aren't like dogs," Charlotte said. "You can't say 'Sic 'em' or 'Go fetch' and have cats do it. I try to keep Moses out of your ma's sight."

Phronny nodded. "I'll help you watch him, and I'll scare Moses away from our camp before Mamma sees him anytime he comes near," she promised.

Moses was on the wagon seat when Charlotte reached camp with the water. He jumped down to rub against her ankles, purring a welcome. Charlotte stooped to scratch him between the ears.

"Oh, Moses, I do wish I could shut you up in a cage, like the chickens," she said.

"Now, why in the world would you want to do that?" Mrs. Van Antwerp exclaimed, patting Moses. "Cats never have been beasts to take to confinement, and Moses is as independent a cat as I've ever seen—and as dependable, too, for that matter."

Charlotte told her about Captain Warren's threat. Mrs. Van Antwerp pursed her lips and bent over the stove.

"Now, Charlotte," she said finally, "why don't you run off and get cool in the creek? Worrying isn't going to do Moses a snippet of good—or you, either. Right now, while you are cooling off, you can do a good turn by keeping an eye on the little ones so their mothers are free to do their washing. Scamper!"

Charlotte removed her shoes. She ran to the creek and waded into the pool until the cool water was tickling around her knees. Enjoying the clean cold after the gritty heat of the trail, she watched the never-ending procession of wagons.

Essie Turner, holding her skirts high to keep them dry, splashed out to stand beside Charlotte. With a frown puckering her thin face she watched the steady stream of prairie schooners.

"They'll get to Oregon before us!" she announced in a mournful tone. "My pa doesn't hold with this stoppin' just to do a batch of wash. Look, just look at them. They're goin' to get there before we do. That's what my pa says."

Worriers and complainers! That's all the Turners were, except Dan. Charlotte could not think of anything to say to Essie. Then seeing Midge and Lettie, their faces streaked with dust, Charlotte waded toward the bank.

"Come on," she urged Essie. "Let's take Midge and Lettie wading so they can cool off, too."

Taking the little girls by the hand, Charlotte led the way to the shallows where they would be safe. They spent the rest of the afternoon splashing, wading, sailing boats, and making forts in the sand.

"Can we play, too?" asked Phronny, leading Alice into the shallows.

Charlotte was grateful for Phronny's company. Essie soon grumbled, "Mud pies and boats, that's babyish." She wandered back to the wagon, where her mother let her rock Peter-Paul.

When the supper calls sounded, Charlotte dried her feet and hands on the grass. She noticed with surprise that the sky had darkened. Angry clouds towered up in the west and spilled over to cover the whole sky. It was hot and breathless and still. Every group along the weary road to Oregon had gone into its circle for the night, so the trail was quiet for the first time since sunrise.

"It doesn't seem natural without wagon wheels groaning," Charlotte said as she ate her beans and salt pork. "It's so still."

"It's the world-stillness before a summer storm—it's not just there being no wagons," Mrs. Van Antwerp said. "Maybe the storm will hold off. Bert and Reuben want you to go with them across the creek about a quarter of a mile where they've found some blackberry bushes."

"Oh, yummy!" exclaimed Charlotte. "Blackberry pie!"

"It'll have to be cobbler," Ma cautioned. "I can't spare all the shortening a pie would take. But even cobbler will be a treat to liven up our biscuits. Don't wander too far, and keep an eye on the boys and on the storm. It wouldn't do for you to get caught over there on the other side of the creek."

In high spirits Charlotte took a pail to fill with berries. She followed Bert and Reuben toward the creek. They stopped at the Warren camp to invite Lucy and Phronny to go with them. Captain Warren brightened at mention of berries, but Mrs. Warren, fearful of the storm, forbade Phronny and Lucy to go. Charlotte and the boys went on, leaving Lucy and Phronny with mournful faces.

Moses jumped out of the bushes beside the creek just as Charlotte balanced herself on the first of the stepping-stones. She stopped and lifted him to her shoulder.

"You'll have to be very good," she told him, "and not wander while I pick berries."

"You talk to that silly cat like you would to a person," Reuben scoffed. "You can't even talk to a dog that way, and dogs are smarter than cats."

"Oh, I don't know about that," Charlotte argued. "This

cat is extra-specially smart."

They had reached the blackberry vines up the creek and across a little hill that hid them from the camp. Charlotte set Moses on the ground. He crouched, quivering and starting at every cricket or grasshopper. He crept through the blackberry patch, slapping down grasshoppers, eating them in one gulp. He found a fat field mouse and played with it for a while before he ate it, but he stayed close to Charlotte.

"Stop eating berries," Reuben warned Charlotte as he stopped to rest, "or you'll not have any to take back to camp. My ma says it's a sin the way you love that cat. Love's for people, she says."

"Then I guess I'm just a sinner," said Charlotte calmly. "I saved his life, and then he saved my life—and I do love him, so there."

Reuben popped a handful of berries into his mouth and jerked Charlotte's braid with berry-stained fingers. "So there! So there!" he said with a laugh. "We'll just have to tell my ma that you can love a cat with cat-love and love your folks with people-love at the same time. But better keep Moses out of Ma's sight now, because . . ."

A loud clap of thunder overhead blurred Reuben's words. He reached for Charlotte's hand and pulled her toward camp. "We better make a run for it," he said.

Charlotte jerked away from him and snatched up Moses. Thunder roared overhead, and the rain came down like a solid wall of water. Stumbling, Charlotte made her way to the boys. They were already drenched.

A tongue of lightning darted from the sky and split a large oak tree just beyond the blackberry patch. The noise was deafening, and the children fell to their knees, holding their ears. Moses dug his claws into Charlotte's shoulder and clung to her.

There was no lightning for a moment. Clutching hands again, Charlotte and the boys made their way toward the creek. Charlotte was panting. They seemed to slip back almost as many steps as they went forward.

Bert, who was leading the way, stopped with a cry. Charlotte pushed up against him. She gasped. How could they ever reach camp? A watery chaos spread out before them. The creek had flooded its banks. It had grown into a raging river and now it foamed close to their feet. Spreading wide on the other side, it engulfed the Warren camp in a swift flood.

Charlotte looked for the Van Antwerp wagon and tent on the far edge of the camp. The tent was upright, but it stood in a pond. The stained wagon cover had held firmly through the wind. Looking at the rest of the camp, Charlotte saw that the laundry over which the women had worked so hard all afternoon was blown and scattered about. Trees and bushes that had been covered with drying clothes were empty. The creek swept away clothing and sheets, bobbing them out of reach.

Clutching hands and speechless, Charlotte, Bert, and Reuben slowly started down the hill. The rain was a drizzle now. Snakes of lightning flashed far off in the east, and the thunder grumbled in the distance. The sky was brightening, and the sun shone through the few clouds left on the western horizon.

"Look," exclaimed Reuben in relief, "there's Pa."

Across the creek stood Captain Warren. With him were Mrs. Van Antwerp, Mr. Smithers, and old Mr. Johnson. Bert raised his arm and shouted. The men ran toward their horses, mounted, and rode into the creek.

The horses picked their way through the muddy water. The children waded to meet them. Reuben climbed up behind Mr. Smithers. Bert swung up behind Mr. Johnson. Captain Warren bent down and pulled Charlotte up in front of him. In the confusion Moses growled and slipped from Charlotte's arms. She turned, reaching down for the cat, but Captain Warren urged his horse ahead. Somewhere in the wet grass Moses hid.

Mrs. Van Antwerp unpacked dry clothing for Charlotte and Bert. "Count yourselves lucky," she told them. "Many a boy and girl in camp saw their only change of clothes washed away."

Although the Van Antwerps were lucky to have dry clothing and bedding, and food supplies untouched by the water, the rush of the flood had carried away their crate of chickens. And Moses was gone.

Charlotte thought she'd gladly remain wet, if only Moses and the chickens were safe.

Before they slept, the whole camp moved to higher ground away from the creek. It was a miserable night. Blankets and bedding had been soaked through. Wood was wet and no one could start a fire.

In the morning the women took inventory. The storm had broken so suddenly that some provisions had not been covered in time. Many families lost flour or sugar or supplies of bread. Charlotte's shoes were missing.

The storm ended the heat. The sky was clear.

Mrs. Van Antwerp started a fire with a bundle of dry twigs hidden under the wagon seat. It was the only fire in the whole camp circle, so Ma rolled up her sleeves and made hot cakes for everyone. Mr. Smithers took the griddle

when Ma began to look flushed and tired. He tossed the browning hot cakes and skillfully flipped them.

When no one could eat another mouthful Mr. Smithers' hound dog wolfed down the hot cakes that were left. Watching him, Charlotte blinked back tears of longing for Moses. She looked toward the creek, wishing that she could go across to look for her kitten. But Mr. Alden was standing with his Bible open in his hands for Sunday services. He was never at a loss to find something to describe their lot in life. He read about Noah and his family and all the creatures in the ark that survived the flood. When he read about the Children of Israel crossing the Red Sea, he paused to smile over his glasses at Bert and Reuben and Charlotte. He read the story that Jesus told about the house built on sand, "and the rain descended and the floods came." And from the Psalms he read, "The Lord sitteth upon the flood."

At last Mr. Alden said, "And in the Song of Songs, we see this, and best we'd not forget it: 'Many waters cannot quench love, neither can the floods drown it.' "

He stopped and Charlotte thought, Oh, I do love Mr. Alden. He is like Pa, always finding pretty words to fit things.

91

Captain Warren started to pray. He prayed for a long time, and then the worship was over. Men stood quietly talking while the women returned to their wagons.

Reuben jogged up on his pony with Phronny sitting beside him. "Get your old horse, Bert," Reuben said. "Pa wants us to go down the creek to see if we can find any of the laundry and things that washed away in the flood. Phronny wants Charlotte to go, too."

They went as far as the ford, a half mile below camp. Reuben retrieved several shirts and a blanket. Bert found the empty chicken crate, battered and useless, caught in the willows below the ford. He took it apart and tied the slats in a bundle.

"We can dry them out and they'll come in handy for kindling," he said quietly.

"Those beautiful chickens all gone," mourned Charlotte. "I did so want to start our Oregon chicken yard with hens from Wisconsin."

"And think of the chicken and dumplings you could have eaten on the way," said Reuben. "And all those eggs you won't have. The eggs my ma packed are all gone."

"There'll be chicken yards in Oregon," Bert said sensibly. "And we can always shoot a prairie chicken for dumplings. I guess we'll just have to learn to get along without eggs. Come on, we'd better get back."

Charlotte looked about for Moses, but she hardly knew where to begin.

Monday morning, trail routines took up their old pattern for the Warren train. But Charlotte missed Moses, who always bounded in from the prairie at the crack of the pilot's rifle. She missed the chickens cackling and complaining under the wagon.

Mr. Smithers led the way downstream to a new ford, still high and roiled. Everyone crossed safely and cautiously through the water. All went well until Mr. Brown urged his teams into the stream. The wagon bumped, lurched, and came to a stop with a grating sound and a splintering of wood. The Brown children cried out, and men from the wagons already across rushed to the water's edge. Mr. Brown stared down in dismay as the wagon tilted crazily in the muddy water. He had driven against a boulder, submerged in the high water. The front axle was broken.

Hurrying back from the head of the train, Captain Warren paused at the muddy ford, scratched his head, and turned back to the other wagons.

"Circle again," he ordered briskly. "We'll camp right here until we get it fixed."

"Well!" exclaimed Mrs. Van Antwerp when their wagon was in place in the circle. "This will be a fine chance for you, Charlotte and Lucy, to get on with your studies. I'll set a rising of yeast bread. We'll enjoy that when the wagon's repaired."

Loud, angry voices broke out from the men gathered around the Browns' tilted wagon, dragged from the water with the help of extra teams of oxen. Mr. Turner was waving his fist in the air as he shouted, "I tell you, it's just Brown's hard luck. Why should the rest of us hold back because of that?"

"Seems like we ought to stick together. We started that way," suggested Mr. Martin, who usually had little to say.

Charlotte listened at the edge of the group. Mr. Harris and his two big sons joined the Turners, arguing that the rest of the train should go on.

"It's Brown's hard luck, not mine," Mr. Harris said in a

surly tone. He kicked a stone toward the creek.

Captain Warren drew himself up to his full height. His voice was soft, but it carried across the suddenly quiet camp. "I think Martin is right. We are in this together. Those who are in such a hurry to get on are free to go. But the only way the rest of us can go is to abandon that broken wagon. We will have to share space and take the Browns into our wagons."

Charlotte gasped. What wagon had room to take on the Browns? There were eight of them, Mr. and Mrs. Brown and six noisy, bouncy, long-legged children.

Mrs. Van Antwerp came to join Charlotte. She put her arm around Charlotte's shoulders for a moment. Looking at Ma's calm face and smiling eyes, Charlotte decided that there was nothing to worry about.

Mr. Harris, whose wagon was overflowing with his own family of eight children, and Mr. Turner who had six children, now suddenly examined the broken axle.

Very businesslike, Mr. Harris (who had been a blacksmith in Tennessee) crawled under the tilting wagon to determine what to do. He called out orders that were quickly followed by the anxious men.

While the men struggled with problems of blacksmithing in the wilderness without a real forge or proper tools, the women brought out mending or scoured a blackened skillet or puttered at wagon-cleaning.

All day long the steady stream of covered wagons lumbered past them. Finally toward evening the repairs on the Brown wagon were finished. As suppers were ladled out from kettles or skillets around the camp circle Mrs. Van Antwerp opened the Dutch oven and took out plump loaves of bread.

Charlotte ran to several wagons with a loaf for each family. She hurried to the Warrens' wagon, shifting the hot loaf from one hand to the other. Mrs. Warren suddenly gave a scream. A little black creature leaped in front of Captain Warren and brushed against Charlotte's legs. It bounded across the camp and disappeared into the Van Antwerp wagon, seconds ahead of Mr. Smithers' hound dog.

Charlotte thrust the loaf of bread into Lucy's hands and ran to her own wagon. There was Moses panting on his bed under the seat. He was too wet and mud-splattered to be cuddled. Scratching him under the chin, Charlotte whispered, "Oh, you precious kitty."

Then she stopped to listen, for Captain Warren was talking to her mother. "I thought the flood had solved that problem," he was saying. "I thought we had lost that cat for good without having to take steps to get rid of him."

"Had you really felt that was necessary?" Mrs. Van Antwerp asked. Charlotte, listening, shivered at her icy tone.

"Why, I don't see how you could expect me to think anything else!" the man answered.

"Captain Warren," Mrs. Van Antwerp said, her voice suddenly gentle, "Moses is a harmless cat. At home on the farm he was the best mouser and the sweetest pet we ever had."

"I don't agree with you that he is harmless," Captain Warren declared. "Mrs. Warren is too delicate to be startled as she was just now, and she objects to the children, especially Alice, lolligagging with a dirty animal. One more disturbance and that animal has to go."

The captain stalked away. Shocked silence filled the camp. Charlotte stood in the back of the wagon to watch him go. Beyond him she saw Phronny, her hand clapped over her mouth, her frightened eyes searching and finding Charlotte in the wagon.

When Captain Warren had disappeared into the wagon, Essie Turner darted across the circle to stand before Charlotte. "My ma always said having truck with a black cat is bad luck," she said.

Charlotte's voice trembled. "My pa always says talk about black cats is just superstition, and superstition is just ignorance, and sensible people don't give it any heed."

Mrs. Turner joined Essie and threatened, "Don't you spout that ignorance-talk to me and my young ones. You'll be talking out of the other side of your face when you get kicked out of this train. You weren't with us at the start. Nothin' says we have to stick with uppity folks like you."

Mrs. Van Antwerp, looking very stern, came to Charlotte to help her make up her bed. "Oh, I do wish Johan were here," she said sighing. "He always knows how to calm the troubled waters of the soul!"

Charlotte undressed, unable to control the tears she had fought back when everyone was watching. Ma knelt beside her for a moment. She looked at Moses as he cleaned his muddy fur. "Now I'm sorry he came back from the flood," said Charlotte, sobbing.

"Why, Charlotte Johanna Van Antwerp!" Ma exclaimed. "I knew you had your faults, but I never dreamed that disloyalty was one of them."

Mrs. Van Antwerp picked up Moses and cuddled him on her lap. With his fur still plastered to his sides he showed his ordeal by flood, but he was clean and glossy. Stretching out on Ma's lap, he purred.

"One thing is certain," Ma said. "We can't expect Moses to be anything but a cat. So it's up to us. We mustn't by any carelessness add to the Captain's worries. And another certain thing is that you can't go 'round telling a girl that her pa's beliefs are ignorance."

"But, Ma, it is just supersti—"

"But me no buts, Charlotte," Ma said quickly. "You are Johan Van Antwerp's daughter. Do as you would be done by, that's your father's creed. Don't be a sharp-tongued perfectionist like me. Every time you feel like giving Essie Turner a piece of your mind, just think of your pa and keep still."

Now Ma smiled as Moses licked her hand. She put him back on his bed and dried her hand against her apron. "I'm glad he came back from the flood. Now you go to sleep and try to forget about Captain Warren's putting us or Moses or anyone out of the train. That's a bridge to cross when we get to it. We'll all help you keep Moses out of sight."

"We'd like to give some of that help," someone said softly just outside the wagon.

Charlotte sat up and saw Mr. Alden in the twilight.

"Mamma and I were just talking," Mr. Alden said, "about what a task Miss Charlotte will have controlling her kitty, cat nature being what it is. I recollected that once when I was a little lad and we had to move, my grandmother told me to smear my kitty's paws with butter. When he's eaten it, she said, he'll decide the new home's best, and there he'll stay!"

" 'Tain't truly like that at all," came the soft voice of Mrs. Alden. "We always smeared our cats with butter, paws and whiskers and all. A cat is a finicky beast. He'll wash and wash to get himself clean, and when he's all clean he's so tuckered out he'll need another nap. By the time he wakes up, he's all out of mind to run away. That's how 'tis!"

Mr. Alden said, "Whichever way 'tis, butter seems to be the answer. So here's our little dish of butter, Miss Charlotte."

Tears brimmed in Charlotte's eyes as she realized that she was probably holding the butter for the Aldens' morning pancakes, made as the churn swung along under the wagon.

"Th-thank you," she stammered, overwhelmed at their kindness.

As the Aldens moved away hand in hand, Mr. Smithers appeared at the other side of the wagon.

"Ev'nin'," he said. He paused to shoot a stream of tobacco juice off into the dust. "If I was as good at sermonizin' as I am at train-breakin', I'd tell Charlotte not to make a mountain out of a molehill. Because it's honest truth, and let it comfort her, a cat with one eye that's green and one eye that's blue is pure good luck."

Charlotte lay quietly in the wagon for a few moments, listening to the evening sounds in camp. Her mother stretched out beside her.

"Do you suppose Mr. Smithers is right?" Charlotte asked as she tickled Moses.

"Right about not making mountains out of molehills? Of course he's right," Ma said, sounding drowsy.

"No, I mean about odd eyes," Charlotte said.

"Black cats, bad luck . . . odd-eyed, good luck. It's all superstition, Sharlie, and it was you who said that superstition is ignorance, remember?"

At the crack of the sentinel's rifle before sunrise next morning, Moses rose and stretched. He was ready to jump to the ground for his usual early morning hunt. Charlotte grasped him firmly. He struggled and mewed, but she held him while she smeared his face with the Aldens' butter, plastering his handsome whiskers to his face. She daubed some on his front paws, too.

"There, you rascal," Charlotte said. "You are really important to get so much butter. I haven't had that much on my pancakes for weeks. But we must keep you out of Captain Warren's sight."

She put the cat down and hurriedly pulled on her dress. She was late to join her mother for her morning chores. Moses shook all four paws emphatically, one at a time, to express his distaste for the messy turn of affairs. As Charlotte hastily smoothed her hair and jumped from the wagon, Moses retreated to his bed and started the task of cleaning himself. He was still sprawled out, cleaning, when Charlotte climbed to her place on the seat at starting time.

The wagon train was ready to move when a group of Indians galloped up. One look at their dogs, and Moses hid in the wagon box.

These Indians were taller and darker than the Indians Charlotte had known on the shores of Lake Winnebago. Trailing behind the men came women on little ponies.

Babies bounced along in cocoon-like sacks on carrying boards strapped to their mothers' backs. Several women had children sitting behind them on the ponies. Each pony pulled a travois made of skins fastened to a frame stretched between two saplings.

Many of the children and women of the Warren group retreated inside their wagons as Moses had done. Charlotte and her mother stood together by their dying fire while Mr. Smithers talked with the Indians and translated for Captain Warren. The Indians were surly, sensing unfriendliness. They helped themselves to a piece of corn bread here, a tool there.

Mrs. Van Antwerp stepped forward and smiled. "Welcome, friends!" she said slowly, as she had always greeted the Indians on their spring and fall visits to the farm. The surly look left the Indians' faces as they softened a little. One man replied, "Friend!"

The Indian who had spoken reached for a portion of corn bread still in the pan. Mrs. Van Antwerp held up her hand to halt him. Charlotte's throat tightened as she watched her mother.

"Swap?" Ma asked, and she indicated Charlotte's bare feet.

The Indian stared at Ma for a moment, then at Charlotte's bare toes. The man turned and went to a travois. He returned to Mrs. Van Antwerp with a pair of beaded mocassins.

"Swap?" he said.

Smiling, Mrs. Van Antwerp handed him the corn bread and gave Charlotte the mocassins. Then the Indian saw the little mirror hung over the whip-holder on the front of the wagon where Mrs. Van Antwerp combed her hair—the

mirror Mrs. Pennywell had impulsively handed Ma on that last morning near Lake Winnebago. The Indian took it and studied his own face. He laughed and turned to Ma, extending the mirror.

"Swap!" he demanded.

Charlotte held her breath. It was their only mirror and a memento of a dear friend, but Ma did not hesitate.

"Swap!" she agreed as heartily as if swapping were her greatest joy in life. "Meat? Buffalo?"

The man returned to the travois and brought Ma a bundle of dried meat. Ma handed him the mirror and took the meat. She smiled at him and then shook his hand.

"Thank you," Ma said. "Good swap!"

"Good swap!" he agreed. Each of the Indian men shook hands with Mrs. Van Antwerp and Charlotte. Then they went to their horses, mounted, and the whole group rode off toward the southwest.

Everyone rushed to the Van Antwerp wagon to examine the mocassins and to look at the dried meat.

"But how did you dare?" Mrs. Wells asked. "And he took your mirror, too. I don't own a mirror myself."

"Nor do I any longer," said Mrs. Van Antwerp, with a laugh. "But I do have a good piece of dried buffalo meat for a stew tonight."

"If I bring a bit of parsnip and some potatoes and some onions, ma'am," said Mr. Smithers, "maybe you'll invite us to partake of your stew. And now, if we don't get started, we'll not make it to the Platte by noonin', as I had calc'lated to do."

There was a rush for the wagons. The words "Platte River" had almost a magic sound to the tired travelers. With mocassins to protect her feet, Charlotte was glad to walk along beside the trail. Essie Turner and Lucy Warren came to walk with her.

"Mamma is still crying because of the Indians," said Lucy. "How could your mother stand there and talk to them and trade with them? How did she think of swapping? Didn't you just about die of fright?"

"No—o—," Charlotte said. "I was sort of frightened. I didn't know these men, and I am always a bit scared of strangers. But we traded with our Indian neighbors at home, so I wasn't really very scared."

Essie shivered. "My pa says there's no good Indian but a dead Indian. Why ever did you shake hands with them?"

"Oh, for goodness' sake!" exclaimed Charlotte. "There are good Indians and bad Indians, just like there are good white men and bad white men. Pa always told Johnny and Bert and me that we were latecomers, living on the Indians' land by the leave of the Indians. And he said if we were impolite to them, he'd give his willow switch a good work-out on us. We always shook hands when they came to our house. But I was afraid Ma'd swap Moses for a dog!"

Charlotte and Phronny and Lucy ran ahead of the lead wagon and so they had the first view of the Platte River, spread out below them for miles and miles.

On the far bank of the wide shallow river was another line of wagons, almost as long as the continuous procession that included the Warren party. So wide was the valley that the wagons on the far side looked almost like toys.

Charlotte started to count them aloud, "And twenty-one, twenty-two, twenty-three . . ."

She stopped. Such a multitude of people, she thought to herself, all making their way along the trail to Oregon.

Mr. Smithers was walking his horse the length of the

Warren train, directing the wagons to a cutoff trail through low sandy hills.

"We'll take our rest in that clump o' cottonwoods next to the river," he said.

"And then will we cross the Platte?" asked Charlotte.

"And be in Oregon at last?" added Phronny.

Mr. Smithers shifted his wad of tobacco. "Oregon? Bless you, no! A thousand miles at least before you're in Oregon, missy. Why, we're only three hundred sixteen miles out from Independence. A sight closer to home than to Oregon. And we ain't crossing yet. Hundred miles or more, we'll stick to the south bank till we get to a river that's sane and crossable."

"What's the matter with the river?" asked Phronny. "Why don't you like the other side?"

"T'other side's not got grass enough for all the stock," he explained. "And that river—it ain't exactly deservin' the name of river. A mile wide and only six inches deep. Not exactly got water in it, neither. The stuff's too thick to drink and too thin to plow. Along through here, you can't safely ford because o' quicksand."

The Platte River had been their goal for so many days. Now it spread out wide, shallow, and shifting, always in sight just to the north of them.

"I feel disappointed inside," Charlotte confided to her mother at lunch as she held Moses. "Nothing's different."

Her mother handed her a dampened handkerchief. Holding it lightly over her nose and mouth, she had some protection from the dust-filled air. It settled so heavily on everything that Charlotte could not see the lead wagon of their own train. Her throat and nose felt raw, and her red-rimmed eyes watered.

"You're feeling letdown," her mother said. "Look toward Oregon, not toward the Platte, nor Fort Laramie. Just Oregon, and nothing in-between."

At nooning came word that while the dust was so bad, the last wagon was to lead off first to make a change. As they took their position at the head of the line, Charlotte looked around, expecting to see the Turners. But the Turners were busy at their own wagon.

The last wagon of the next train was far enough ahead so that for the first time in days Charlotte and her mother were free of dust as they rode.

"I believe I'll crawl back with Moses and take a snooze myself," said Mrs. Van Antwerp, after nodding and dozing on the seat. "You stay here to call me if anything goes wrong. They drive themselves, really. Nip's the one you have to watch. Just snap the whip over his head, like this. He'll behave. I've never had to whip them."

The hot afternoon dragged on. At first Charlotte brandished the whip grandly and wished some of the other children could see her driving the head wagon of the train. But all who could were napping inside the wagons.

Charlotte was glad when the call sounded to stop for the night. Her mother crawled from the hot wagon to guide the oxen into the camp circle. Charlotte set up the stove, started the fire, and put pieces of salt pork to fry while her mother joined the people talking with Captain Warren at the Turners' wagon.

Charlotte was still alone when Bert, solemn-faced and hot from rounding up the animals for the night, came for his supper.

"Dan's mother and baby brother are sick," Bert told her. "Dan and I have to ride ahead to see if there's a doctor.

105

Ma says you're to go on and eat and get things ready for the night."

Trail fever! Every time they had passed a fresh grave along the way, Charlotte and Ma had clasped hands tightly for a moment.

"Just thank God we're well," Ma said each time. "And thank Him, too, that we had our good, wise Johan to warn us about boiling every drop of water we drink."

"Bert," Charlotte said, pushing away her plate of supper untouched, "it's the Turners who are sick, and Mrs. Turner was the only one who wouldn't take Ma's word. She always said that boiling water was too much bother. Oh, how sick little Peter-Paul must be!"

Bert nodded. He and Dan had become good friends in the night watches and along the trail. Dan's grief was Bert's grief, too. Bert ate hastily and then went to meet Dan.

"Remember, Sharlie," Bert called as he and Dan started up the trail to the west, "you're to get camp in order for the night. Ma may not get back to sleep."

When she had washed the dishes, put the campfire out, and had the bedrolls ready, Charlotte sat forlornly on the wagon tongue. She had let Moses stray a little way and now called him back. The quiet in the camp was almost frightening.

Each train that passed was stopped by Mr. Smithers. "Any doctor in your group?"

Always the answer was No. Wagons hurried on faster, for everyone was afraid of trail fever, the dread cholera.

Darkness fell and Charlotte crept into the wagon to go to bed. Undressed, she stayed at the back opening of the wagon. A prairie wolf howled. There was an uneasy stirring among the animals. Peter-Paul cried.

106

Charlotte awoke when Bert and Dan returned with the doctor from a train ahead. He left medicines with Mrs. Van Antwerp to help Mrs. Turner, but he was too late to help little Peter-Paul. He rode away to join his own train only at the crack of the watchman's rifle in the early morning light.

After breakfast, Mr. Smithers and Mr. Johnson went to a little glade in the cottonwood trees with their shovels, but Dan Turner, white and sad faced, came after them. "He's my little brother. I'd be proud to make his last little bed," Dan said. And so Dan dug the grave.

Everyone stood quietly while Mr. Alden opened his worn Bible and read, "In my Father's house are many mansions . . . ." Captain Warren prayed. No one was ashamed of wet eyes.

When they covered the little grave, Dan and Bert rolled a boulder from the riverbed to place on top of the loose earth.

"I'm hoping," Dan said, "that Peter-Paul will sleep in peace."

Dan brought a brush and tar bucket, and painted on the boulder in wobbly, uneven letters:

PETER-PAUL TURNER
JULY 15, 1852

As the train resumed its way, Charlotte urged her mother, "You go back with Moses and rest. I'm turning into a first-rate driver. Pa'd never forgive me if I let you work too hard and you got sick."

Mrs. Van Antwerp went gratefully. That morning set the pattern for the many to follow. Once the fever had entered the Warren train, it went from one wagon to another. The Turners all sickened before Mrs. Turner was

107

strong enough to care for them. Only the Aldens and the Van Antwerps remained well.

With the medicines the doctor had given her, and with the knowledge of nursing that she had learned from her husband, Mrs. Van Antwerp became the ministering angel to the whole Warren group. No one else died, but everyone was to remember those miles up the south bank of the Platte as the most wretched days of their lives.

Charlotte wondered if Oregon was a goal never to be reached by anyone.

11

One hot July evening Charlotte walked to the herders' fire with a packet of johnny-cake for the boys' midnight lunch. Reuben was playing with Old Red, the sheep dog.

"Don't you wish your pet was a dog?" Reuben asked. "Then he could earn his way to Oregon and my father'd not have a word to say, nor my ma, either, because she's not afraid of dogs."

Charlotte turned and walked back to her wagon, wishing Captain Warren did not expect everyone and everything to be of use.

Reaching into the wagon for the leash made from two sunbonnet strings knotted together, Charlotte snapped her fingers to call Moses. With the leash tied to a little collar Bert made from a bit of old bridle, Charlotte could give Moses some exercise each night.

Now he rubbed against Charlotte's legs, purring as if to say, "This is a bad business, but we love each other and we're in it together."

He took off so rapidly toward a rise of ground beyond the herders' fire, that Charlotte lost the leash for a moment. She had to run to catch it again. Moses galloped in and out among little mounds of earth. He sniffed at one mound and then another. Suddenly out of the mounds popped little squirrel-like heads. The animal nearest Charlotte started

109

yipping at Moses and then popped back into the safety of his hole, while another, a few feet away, took up the scolding.

Charlotte and Moses were in the midst of a prairie dog town!

The hysterical barking of the prairie dogs attracted the attention of Old Red, the Turners' Brownie, the Hoods' Old Buck, and Mr. Smithers' hound dog. The dogs raced toward the prairie dog town yapping and bellowing.

The whole camp was instantly aroused. Mr. Smithers, Mr. Sawyer, and Captain Warren came running.

Charlotte picked up Moses, who spat at the dogs. Mr. Smithers and Mr. Sawyer laughed and returned to their fires when they learned that nothing was attacking the camp, but Captain Warren stalked along beside Charlotte.

"I might have known it was that cat behind the uproar," he said. "I am a just man. I'll not put your pet out of the way this time because I can't show that any real damage

was done. But I'm warning you, as the trail grows rougher and the way grows harder, mind your step, young lady, you and your pet."

"Yes, sir. Yes, Captain Warren," Charlotte said faintly, tucking Moses under her arm away from the captain.

She climbed into the wagon and reached for the little dish of butter. She plastered Moses, paws and face and proud whiskers.

Mrs. Van Antwerp was sitting up with feverish Phronny, for with Mrs. Warren's baby to be born very soon, everyone was taking a share of the work to help out. Charlotte cried herself to sleep in the lonely wagon.

Deep in the night, still far from sunrise but long after fires had burned away to ashes, Charlotte was wakened by the weight of Moses, tense and heavy on her middle. He was growling at something out in the blackness.

Charlotte arose and, holding Moses tightly in her arms, peered out into the dark. Nothing moved in the Warren

camp. No wolves howled across the river. But suddenly Charlotte heard the frightening sound that had roused Moses.

It was a low, steady roar that filled her ears and shook the earth beneath her. It seemed impossible, but no one stirred in the entire camp. Even the herders slept.

Baffled by the sound but certain it was full of danger, Charlotte hid Moses in a fold of her nightgown. Someone must be roused. If she called out, they would only think she was talking in her sleep.

Stumbling over the ground, she came upon the first sleeper, Mr. Smithers, rolled in his blanket before the ashes of his fire. Charlotte shook him.

"Mr. Smithers, wake up! Listen!"

He was instantly alert and on his feet. The roar could mean only one thing. He fired his rifle into the air, calling, "Warren! Johnson! Harris! Brown! Quick. A stampede—buffalo—a whole herd comin' right our way!"

The men of the camp jumped from wagons or threw aside blankets beside their smoldering campfires. Guns in their hands, they ran toward Mr. Smithers.

"Children, stay in the wagons," Mr. Smithers ordered, pushing Charlotte back toward her wagon. "Ladies, build a whole row of fires, fast as ye can! Right to the south of the wagons. Herders, inside the circle with our animals—hurry! Men, come with me!"

The roar in the dark grew louder. The herders and dogs had all they could do to drive the nervous animals into the hollow circle formed by the wagons.

It seemed that the little circle of sixteen wagons was about to be engulfed by the ominous noise. Suddenly out of the vibrating darkness just beyond the range of the flickering light of the fires there came six rifle shots. They were puny sounds against the onrushing roar of the stampeding, bellowing buffalo herd—feeble sounds, yet positive. There was a change, a hesitation, an interruption in the rhythm of the pounding hooves.

It was moments before Charlotte realized what had happened. Something out there in the dark had caused a pause in the onrush of the buffalo. When the rhythm of the stampede resumed, the herd had split into two parts, one part passing to the left of the camp, the other to the right.

Within the circle of the wagons, the oxen, cows, mules, horses, Mr. Brown's sheep, and Mr. Well's goats were hard to control and milled constantly. Bert and Dan did their best to calm them.

By daylight the last buffalo lagging at the rear of the herd had disappeared downriver.

As the women stirred up the fires to start breakfast, the men returned, dusty and red eyed, carrying dressed buffalo meat and the hides of six buffalo to cure.

Mrs. Warren threw herself weeping into Captain Warren's arms. "Oh, my darling, my dear! You are safe. What miracle did you perform in the dark to make those dreadful beasts part like the waters of the Rea Sea and leave us safe?"

Captain Warren kissed her and gently led her to her rocker before the campfire. Everyone well enough to be up crowded around to hear the story.

"None of my doing," Captain Warren said. "Let Smithers tell you. It was his miracle."

"No miracle on my part," Mr. Smithers said. "Only thing to do is check 'em in their rush or it's good-bye to whatever's in their path. We checked 'em by shootin' their leaders. The dead critters in their path and the fires burnin' round the wagons made 'em pause just long enough to split 'em into two groups and leave us safe in the middle."

"Thank the Lord for our salvation," intoned Mr. Alden, and everybody called, "Amen!"

"What does beat me, though," Mr. Smithers continued, "is what a narrow escape we had. If we'd been five minutes later in wakin' we couldn't have stopped 'em in time. It's thanks to little Miss Charlotte, here, that we're all alive to tell the tale. How come you heard 'em comin' and the rest of us sleepin' on?"

Charlotte stammered as everyone stared at her. "I—I—I didn't hear them, either. It was Moses. He woke me . . . and—and then, I knew it wasn't right . . . I—I didn't know what it was, but I—I knew I had to get you or Captain Warren or someone quick."

Mr. Smithers shook his head and scratched his whiskers. He shifted his wad of tobacco and aimed a long shot of tobacco juice into the dust. Then he said, "Wal, now! It does seem as if that little black feller has some use to him, doesn't it?"

With buffalo meat to relieve the steady diet of salt pork and six shaggy hides to be cured, the travelers felt their spirits rise. The excitement of the buffalo stampede had given everyone something new to talk over.

In his years as hunter and trapper Mr. Smithers had picked up many useful bits of Indian lore. Now he showed the women how to make jerky out of the buffalo meat that could not be eaten immediately. He had Mr. Harris make a large wooden rectangle, something like an oversized picture frame. Poles were laid across, and the women lifted the frame on teetery legs over a smudge fire.

Mr. Sawyer, who had been a butcher in Maine before he caught the Western fever, cut the buffalo meat into thin slices. The women hung the meat over the poles to cure in the smoke. During the night the herders tended the fire and kept it smoking, and in the morning the jerky was divided among all the families.

The women strung the partly cured strips of meat on ropes as the wagons jolted along the trail. The meat would finish curing as it hung outside the wagons in the hot sun and dry air.

Mrs. Van Antwerp, busy nursing the Warrens, took no part in preparing the jerky, but Charlotte watched with curiosity. She retrieved a small scrap of meat for a tidbit to give Moses.

The Warren family seemed over the worst days of illness, and Mrs. Van Antwerp looked forward to the time when nursing would not be her first concern. But with the new Warren baby expected in only a short time, it was hard for Mrs. Warren to climb up and down into the wagon. More than once she said to Mrs. Van Antwerp, "What a blessed day it will be when the baby is safe in my arms and

Alice is able to skip about again."

Captain Warren was not the kind of man to thank Mrs. Van Antwerp easily for her help, but his expression became less tense as he saw his family recovering. He agreed that it would be a good change for Lucy to ride with Charlotte when the day's journey got underway.

As the Van Antwerp wagon rumbled along, Charlotte and Lucy busied themselves. They strung the strips of partly dried meat on ropes to hang in the hot, still air. Charlotte thought Moses might come prowling around, but the little black cat slept curled in a ball deep in the dark interior of the wagon.

The morning passed quickly, but toward noon the leaders at the front of the train sighted a line of riders in the distance. Indians!

There were many Indians, probably fifty, nearly naked and brightly painted. Their faces were stern, and there was something threatening in their manner even though they rode openly toward the travelers.

Charlotte's heart pounded, but she remained rigid on the seat, grasping the whip so tightly that her knuckles were white.

Lucy could not control her fears. She screamed and dived into the rear of the wagon.

The train paused briefly while Mr. Smithers talked with the Indians. As the Indians rode off, he came toward the Van Antwerp wagon.

"Who's screamin' around here?" he asked sternly. "Them are Sioux and they've just had a fight with a band of Pawnees. Killed plenty of 'em, I guess. None of 'em in a very pleasant mood. If Miss Screamy Warren will just keep her fright to herself, we'll all be better off."

116

Lucy climbed back on the seat beside Charlotte as Mr. Smithers finished. "I'll tell my pa you're speaking disrespectful!" she said.

"No disrespect," he told her angrily. "It's just that I want to see us all through these parts without leavin' corpses or scalps behind."

Lucy shuddered and Mr. Smithers rode away. Suddenly she threw her apron over her face and cried.

Charlotte reached out to comfort Lucy and was astonished when the older girl turned angrily on her. "He's mean and you're just as bad, Charlotte Van Antwerp! Hiding that cat my mother hates and letting him scratch people. Look at my hand! I'll tell Pa—and you know what he'll do!"

Lucy extended her hand and pointed to a faint scratch across the knuckles.

Charlotte's own temper flared. She wanted to shake that ladylike Lucy till her braids tumbled down! But she struggled and controlled herself. If Lucy complained to her father about Moses, nothing could save the little cat.

To release some of her anger Charlotte cracked the whip loudly over the heads of the oxen. They moved a little faster. Lucy caught her breath and looked at Charlotte in surprise.

"I didn't know I could crack it that way," Charlotte said, pleased with herself. Then she reached out and took Lucy's hand. She summoned all her sympathy and said, "I'm awfully sorry he scratched you. Moses really isn't the scratching kind. I guess you scared him when you jumped in the back."

Lucy was not ready to give up. "He shouldn't have been back there at all!" she said. "Pa'd get rid of him in a second . . . ."

117

"I know," Charlotte said. "Can't you see that's why Moses has to stay out of sight? I just wish your father could understand. Moses is a good cat. Suppose he hadn't wakened me before the buffalo stampede?"

"My pa doesn't believe any cat is that smart. He says you woke up because you're a light sleeper."

"Please," Charlotte said. "Please. That scratch will heal fast. If you tell your pa, he'll kill Moses—and Moses will be gone forever. He'll never see his new home and Ma won't have a cat to catch the mice."

Lucy looked thoughtful and finally said, "Well, all right. I won't tell this time."

The wagons halted although it was not time for nooning. The two girls looked anxiously around. Men were conferring at the head of the train. Then Charlotte saw her mother swing down from the Warren wagon and hurry toward the girls.

By now Charlotte was used to seeing her mother look pale and haggard. Nights of nursing and the hardships of the trail had marked Mrs. Van Antwerp's face. But the look there now had nothing to do with these things. Charlotte was frightened. Something had horrified her mother.

"I'm going to drive my own team for a while," Ma said. "Alice is all right and so's your ma, Lucy. You stay right here. I want to talk to both of you girls."

Charlotte waited tensely. What could have happened? But her mother sat silently erect, apparently waiting until she could regain her usual composure before speaking.

One by one the wagons groaned into motion. The oxen moved briskly, as if they sensed a driver who would put up with no foolishness.

Mrs. Van Antwerp cleared her throat and said slowly,

"You saw the Sioux. You know they had a fight with the Pawnees. Up ahead we are going to pass the place where they fought. The Pawnees left their dead behind them. There's no need for you to look at such a sight. Man's meanness to man is never a pretty sight, be the man red or white. Let's close our eyes and say a prayer of our own, 'Thanks, Lord, for our safe deliverance. And forgive us, Lord, for our meanness to each other.' "

Perhaps Mrs. Van Antwerp never guessed the special significance those words had for the two girls on the wagon seat beside her. They closed their eyes and feelingly spoke the little prayer as the wagon jerked along.

How long before she dared look? Charlotte did not know and could not ask. Lucy touched Charlotte with her hand and the two girls felt a new bond of friendship. Silence settled over the whole wagon train.

Charlotte put her arm around Lucy, and then she felt her mother's arms around both girls.

"Have we passed the dead Indians?" Charlotte finally asked. Lucy's regular breathing made Charlotte guess she'd fallen asleep, exhausted.

"Long ago," Ma answered softly, "but I thought the rest would do you both good. I think Lucy should sleep—she's worn out. Remember, when the new baby comes Lucy is going to have to be mother to Phronny and Alice. We'll wake her when we stop."

Time went by slowly and the day grew warmer. Ma said, "Mr. Smithers wants to push on to Cottonwood Spring for a late nooning. Tomorrow we'll move on to ford the river."

Charlotte had heard enough about the ford ahead to feel excited that it was so near. The South Platte was wide and sand-laden, and it could be treacherous, Mr. Smithers often reminded them. She wished that the oxen, especially Sam and Nip, were not so weary. But she pushed gloomy thoughts out of her mind as she glimpsed the green of scrub cedars ahead.

"Lucy, wake up!" Charlotte whispered so as not to startle her. "Trees!"

When the wagons halted, Lucy and Charlotte climbed down and hurried to gather twigs and fallen branches from the cedars that filled the ravines near the spring. As smoke curled up from the cooking fires the girls sniffed it with pleasure. Real wood smoke! For days they had gathered buffalo chips—dried buffalo droppings—to make a poor kind of fire.

Moses mewed to be let out of the wagon. Charlotte longed to scamper among the low cedars with him—but there would be no frolics until the scratch on Lucy's hand had healed.

That night as Charlotte fell asleep she thought of her father and Johnny, far ahead. How had they fared at crossing the Platte? How many miles she had come; how far Oregon still was.

Moses purred softly and Charlotte whispered, "You're lucky. You don't worry about the next day. Right now's all that counts with you."

The South Platte ford at last! Just looking out over the broad river the next morning made Charlotte's heart beat faster. Once safely on the other side she was sure she'd feel much closer to Oregon.

"We'll send the loose animals over first," Captain Warren announced when the wagons had assembled near the ford. "Some of you men will have to stay to guard them, but we'll need all the help we can get to move the wagons across."

Charlotte shaded her eyes and watched Bert as he prodded and pushed the animals toward the water. Some of the cattle waded in gladly enough, but when the full force of the current struck them, panic threatened to take over. The herders did their work well, however, and before long Charlotte saw the first of the cattle climb up on the opposite bank.

Bert was among the group of men and boys who returned to help guide the wagons across. Splashed with water, Bert leaned against the Van Antwerp wagon as it stood in line.

"The river looks so wide," Charlotte said. "Essie Turner says sometimes wagons don't make it."

"Mr. Smithers says it's a lot wider after a rain," Bert said. "It's really not bad after you're in it. What you've got to do is keep moving."

Charlotte was thoughtful. "Bert, the Platte must have been a lot wider in the spring when Pa crossed it. Oh, I hope he's all right!"

"Maybe he didn't even cross here," Bert said. "Mr. Smithers was talking about the Upper California Crossing last night. Maybe Pa crossed there. This is the Lower California Crossing. Or maybe Pa crossed way back where we first came to the Platte. More than one place to cross a river, Sharlie."

Talk stopped because Mr. Smithers was leading the Warren wagon into the river. Bert and Charlotte moved to get a better view. Captain Warren handled his team well. It didn't look so bad after all.

When the Warren wagon was at the first sandbar, Mr. Smithers waved Mr. Johnson into the water, shouting, "Keep the wagons movin'!"

Mr. Harris' turn came next. His team was skittish and the lead animals balked at the drop from the grassy bank into the water. Mr. Harris beat the horses and cursed loudly. The Harris children began to cry. Men and boys ran up, shouting suggestions. Mr. Turner, in place behind the Harrises, fumed and swore at the delay.

The hubbub only added to the trouble. The Warren and Johnson wagons were already approaching the other shore, but the rest of the train was stalled by the Harris team.

Mr. Harris beat his frightened horses, but it was no use. Suddenly Charlotte broke away from the watching crowd and darted toward her own wagon. She had a plan—it might work.

Stooping, she unhooked a pail of oats that hung under the wagon. There was not much left, but she scooped a handful into a pan.

122

"Look, Ma!" she exclaimed. "Maybe Bert can coax Mr. Harris' horses with these oats."

Mrs. Van Antwerp nodded. Bert snatched the pan, mounted his horse, and went back to the riverbank. He spoke quickly to Mr. Smithers, then edged toward the horses' heads. Mr. Harris let his whip drop and held the reins ready as he realized Bert's plan.

Oats! It had been days since the horses had even smelled oats. The crowd grew quiet and the horses moved forward as Bert went a little way out into the water.

"Keep movin'!" Mr. Smithers shouted, and there was no turning back for the Harris wagon. Bert paced the horses to the first sandbar, then turned back.

Now wagon after wagon set forth into the river, fell in with the current, was swept downstream, and then angled back upstream to where the trail began once more.

The Van Antwerp wagon was fifteenth in line. Mr. Smithers was still calling hoarsely, "Keep the wagons movin'!" With Charlotte beside her on the seat, Mrs. Van Antwerp guided the oxen into the water.

All went smoothly, and as the Van Antwerps crossed the first sandbar Mr. and Mrs. Alden followed them into the river, the last of the Warren train.

"We'll make it!" Charlotte whispered under her breath. "Sam and Nip, Tim and Tuck, they'll get us across!" She knew as well as her mother that the huge beasts were under a heavy strain.

Just beyond the sandbar the full strength of the river current seized the animals. The lead team—Sam and Nip—faltered. The wagon lurched, sand slipping away under the iron-rimmed wheels. Sam's head dropped. Behind, the Alden wagon was rapidly overtaking them.

"Keep the wagons movin'!" Mr. Smithers shouted. Astride his horse he drew up even with the Van Antwerp wagon just as Sam struggled and lost his footing.

Bert guided his swimming horse toward Nip's head. Mr. Smithers hurried to free the wagon and Tim and Tuck from the fallen oxen.

"It's this or you'll all go!" he shouted.

Charlotte clung to the wagon seat, trying in spite of her terror to behave as Ma expected her to. She thought her heart would break, though—good old Sam and Nip lost!

Mrs. Van Antwerp clenched her lips and snapped the whip over Tim and Tuck. Bearing the full weight of the wagon, they struggled forward. The water pounded less furiously and became shallower as the wheels hit bottom. They had crossed the Platte!

"God be praised!" Mrs. Van Antwerp exclaimed fervently. But Charlotte saw through her own tears that her mother was crying. Two faithful creatures, a tie with home, were gone forever. Bert rode forlornly ahead. Charlotte knew he was thinking of the miles he had traveled with Nip and Sam.

Charlotte half expected to feel Moses' paw catching at her skirt—he, too, must have been frightened, she thought. But shouts and cries from the river warned her of new trouble.

With the wagon safely on firm land, Charlotte rose from the wagon seat and looked behind her. Theirs was the last wagon! What had become of the Aldens?

"Ma! Where are the Aldens?" she cried. She and her mother jumped down from the wagon and ran to the water. Mr. Smithers was urging his horse up the bank, holding Mrs. Alden in front of him. Dan Turner followed with Mr.

Alden behind him. The four mules that had drawn the Alden wagon were gone. Far out in midstream all that was left of the Alden wagon was a slowly sinking wagon cover.

"Praise the Lord for our salvation!" exclaimed Mr. Alden through chattering teeth, but Mrs. Alden's white face showed too much shock for speech.

The other members of the wagon train gathered around Captain Warren at the river's edge. Speechless in the face of the Aldens' loss, they shaded their eyes to catch a last glimpse of the sinking wagon.

Mr. Smithers pushed back his hat and summed up the losses. "One wagon, four mules, and two oxen less than we began the day with," he said. His face was solemn.

Someone started a fire, and the Aldens stood near it to dry their clothes. Everything they had was gone except the tattered and dripping clothes they wore.

"Here's a shawl," Mrs. Van Antwerp offered. "You're welcome to a place in our wagon." She hugged Mrs. Alden.

"With two of your oxen gone," Captain Warren pointed out, "you'll have to lighten your load, not take on extras." He beckoned to some of the men and they moved off to discuss how best to help.

It was finally decided that the Aldens should go on to Oregon with the Johnsons. Theirs was the largest and finest wagon, with three teams of oxen—all to pull two people. While the Aldens dried themselves near the fire, everyone in the train brought something to make up for their losses—clothing, food, and blankets.

Charlotte brought over what her mother could spare and the Aldens gratefully accepted it.

Mrs. Van Antwerp sighed as she looked at the belongings in the wagon. "It seemed like we were as sparing as a family could be, right from the start," she said. "But we still have a long piece to go, and there's just too much for one team of tired oxen to pull."

But Lottie Van Antwerp was not one to shed tears over what couldn't be helped. She sorted through their few possessions, some of them given by neighbors on the shores of Lake Winnebago. Food was repacked so that a barrel and a chest could be left at the side of the trail. The small plow slung under the wagon was added to the pile. Extra clothing was folded into the bedrolls, and Ma added the little clothes chest to the discard.

Charlotte watched, unable to be of much help. With a wry smile she told herself it was lucky Moses was such a little cat or there'd be no room for him.

At his mother's suggestion Bert took the tar brush and on a rough board lettered "Help yourselves." Thus they left their belongings.

Steadily, day after day, the wagons rolled westward. Many times Charlotte grieved for Tim and Tuck as they strained up steep hills and then braced their legs as they descended, the wagon rattling behind them.

By now the travelers were leaving the flat prairie land behind. The hills rose more steeply and a new danger was added to the trail. The lumbering wagons had no brakes and on a sharp descent could roll out of control.

Mr. Smithers knew how to manage this hazard. At the crest of a hill each wagon was halted and the front and back wheels chained together to stop their turning. This acted like a brake to slow the movement and protect the animals.

One whole day was spent letting the wagons down famous Windlass Hill, one at a time. Heavy ropes restrained each wagon, and men and boys took turns letting the ropes play out little by little until the precious load reached the bottom of the steep drop-off.

Charlotte and the Turner girls, along with Lucy and Phronny, watched till they were tired, then picked their way down over the rocks. With Moses tucked safely in her apron, Charlotte was glad to reach low ground.

The women cast anxious glances in Mrs. Warren's direction. Surely it could not be long before the baby would come. Captain Warren tried to watch out for his wife's well-being, but it was not easy. Perhaps a little to everyone's surprise, Mrs. Warren took the good and the bad as it came. Sometimes it was a delicate-looking woman, like the captain's wife, who proved her real strength on the trail.

When the train camped at Ash Hollow, Mrs. Warren calmly laid out the things for the new baby. During the night Charlotte was roused when Captain Warren called her mother. Although Charlotte strained her ears, she heard no sounds from the Warren wagon, and she finally went to sleep again.

Dawn was pink in the east when Lucy, already dressed, called softly outside the Van Antwerp wagon.

"A baby brother!" she whispered to Charlotte. "We've named him Edgar, after Pa."

"I'm so happy!" Charlotte declared as she hugged Lucy.

Before setting out on the trail the men gathered around Captain Warren, slapping him on the back and congratulating him on his son. Some of the tension was gone from his face—miles lay ahead and many responsibilites, but this milestone had been passed.

"Maybe he'll think more kindly of Moses now," Charlotte said to Bert. "He hasn't so much to worry him."

"Don't count on it," Bert said. "If folks don't like cats at one time, they don't like them another."

And Charlotte had to be satisfied with that.

To relieve the burden for Tim and Tuck, Charlotte walked most of the way every day.

"Atta girl!" Mr. Smithers said one hot morning as he reined in his horse to keep pace with her. "They's rough ways ahead, and it's smart to keep in walkin' trim."

On the days when they were near the end of the train far back from the Warrens, Charlotte let Moses out of the wagon to gambol beside her. He was sleek and glossy, well fed by their friends even when he could not be released to hunt. How different it was for the poor oxen as they plodded wearily along the trail with hooves that bled when the way was rocky.

Time dragged during days when Moses had to remain safely hidden. Those days seemed like the bad dream Charlotte used to have when she was little—a dream of walking, walking until she was tired enough to drop, but never getting anywhere.

Phronny joined her one morning for her first walk since she had been sick. Before they had been walking long there loomed up, far to the left of the trail, what looked like a huge building with many towers and turrets starkly white against the bright blue sky.

"Look! A palace in the wilderness!" Charlotte exclaimed, pointing.

Tears, surprising in the eyes of jolly Phronny, suddenly trickled down her dusty cheeks. "I don't want a palace. I just want a little house!"

Sympathetically Charlotte took Phronny's hand, and they skipped ahead to Mrs. Van Antwerp, who was walking by

Tim and Tuck.

"Is that a palace?" Phronny asked. "Who'd build a palace way out here?"

Mrs. Van Antwerp laughed. "That must be Courthouse Rock. We'll be seeing it most of the day. Watch toward night and see if you can find what some men have called the jailhouse, close to the courthouse."

Through the sunset haze they could see the jailhouse cropping out from the level plain a short distance west of the more imposing Courthouse Rock.

"I don't see how plain rocks can look so much like buildings," Charlotte marvelled.

"Probably if we were close it would seem like just the mass of rock it is," Ma said. "Mr. Smithers says it's all of thirty miles away. Watch out for Chimney Rock tomorrow or the next day. But don't make the mistake of a little boy I heard about, who cried and cried because there wasn't any smoke."

Charlotte and Phronny laughed, but two days later when they saw the tapering finger of black rock towering into the deep blue sky, they could understand the little boy's disappointment, for it did look like a chimney.

Having been fooled so many times by nature's architecture, they could hardly believe their eyes when at last they stood on the plain looking toward Fort Laramie, shining white on a hill, dwarfed by mountains towering behind it. People seemed to swarm like ants around it. Clustered near the fort were Indian tepees. Two emigrant trains were already drawn up in circles across the swift, cold Laramie River where the Warren train had halted, waiting for Mr. Smithers' directions for fording.

When they had ferried the river and selected their camp-

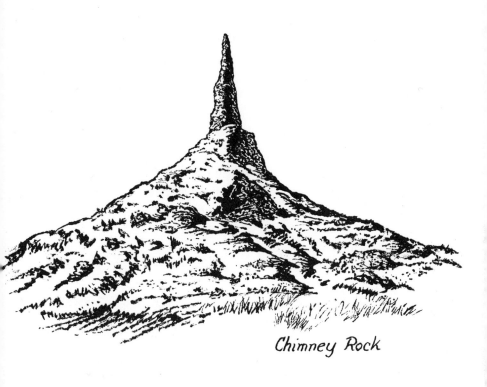

Chimney Rock

site, Mrs. Van Antwerp thoughtfully counted her few coins and surveyed their needs.

"Miles from everywhere like we are, things'll probably cost a fortune," she said. "But Bert's shirt's beyond mending, and Charlotte, you really should have shoes. Here it is the beginning of August. We're going to see snow before we see the Willamette Valley, and those ill-shod feet of yours prey on me."

Charlotte was filled with excitement. Perhaps while she was trying on shoes she might meet someone who had seen Pa, for surely he too had stopped at Fort Laramie.

Then Charlotte was plunged into disappointment when Ma said, "You stay here, Sharlie, and keep an eye on things.

131

Mr. Smithers says thieving is common. Soon as the water's hot, you start the washing. You can do it—you're a careful worker for a girl your size. Bert, you come along to help me carry back the thimbleful I'll be able to buy."

Mother and son walked briskly ahead toward the gates of the fort, unaware of Charlotte's tears. She wiped her sleeves across her eyes, telling herself that she should be proud to be trusted with the family wash.

She scrubbed their trail-worn, dusty garments until her hands were red and blistered. While more water was heating, Charlotte sat on the wagon seat where she could watch everything and wrote a letter to Mrs. Pennywell. Moses curled up on her lap.

"You're no good at all as a writing desk, Moses Van Antwerp," she grumbled, but she scratched him between the ears before she continued her letter—or tried to continue. So much had happened since Fort Kearney on the Fourth of July that she could not find a starting place. As she thought back over the weary miles and endless days, it almost seemed that Fort Laramie was a billion miles from Fort Kearney.

The sun was settling close to the western peaks before Ma and Bert returned. Ma was as cross as Charlotte could remember her being, angry over the high prices at the trading post.

"I'd have to be a landed lord to afford that trader's shoes for my daughter," she scolded, "or his shirts for my son!"

She showed Charlotte what she had bought—a fringed deerskin tunic for Bert and Indian mocassins to replace shoes for all of them.

"I shiver when I think of us trudging through snow in thin mocassins," Ma said ruefully. "But if the Indians live through the snows of winter in mocassins, perhaps we'll survive."

While Ma climbed into the wagon to stow away the beans, salt pork, Indian berry cakes, and smoked venison, Bert came to Charlotte who was bending over the washtub again. He spoke softly, "I looked in the post office to see if Pa had tacked up a letter for us. There are dozens of letters like that, but none from Pa."

Charlotte flashed a grateful smile at Bert, and she said comfortingly, "He doesn't know we're following him so he wouldn't leave us a letter."

"That's right!" Bert exclaimed. "I'd been hoping so hard that we'd hear word of Pa at Fort Laramie, I guess I wasn't using my head right."

Nodding, Charlotte whispered, "I did so want to ask if anyone had talked to him when he passed through."

Bert answered, "I asked everyone who wasn't too busy to talk—but no luck, no luck at all."

Tears brimmed in Charlotte's eyes again. This was worse than not being able to see the fort for herself. Like Bert, she had been hoping, mile after mile, that Fort Laramie would bring news of Pa.

Backing out of the wagon, Ma saw Charlotte's letter waiting to be posted to Mrs. Pennywell.

"Now that's a good idea," she said heartily. "While you make us some supper, Charlotte, I'll write a quick note to my mother and father, and as soon as we've eaten, you and Bert can take them over to the fort. That'll give you a chance to see the sights, too, Sharlie. Mr. Smithers has already said that at sunrise tomorrow we have to be on our way. Goodness knows, my bones could stand another day's rest, but we're so late, so late!"

Charlotte bolted her food and scurried into the wagon to rebraid her hair and put on a clean apron. On impulse she gathered up Moses. Bundling him in her apron so that little of him showed but his perky ears, she joined Bert.

"Aw! Why do you drag him along?" Bert protested.

"Because I love him," Charlotte retorted, "and besides, if I'm not here to watch, he might wander off toward the Warrens' wagon."

Grudgingly Bert agreed, and they walked up the rise of land toward the fort. Moses napped and was no bother at all.

Having posted their letters, the children strolled about the fort. The enclosure was still crowded with soldiers, emigrants, and Indians. Everywhere Bert asked the same polite, anxious question: "Have you by any chance met Dr. Van Antwerp on the trail? He's our pa."

But always the answer was No.

Charlotte's disappointment was deep. The blisters on her hands from the laundry began to smart painfully. Her feet were so tired that she could hardly take one more step, and Moses became a heavy burden. She shifted him to her shoulder as they approached the broad gate of the fort. Wakened by the movement he opened his eyes, and his body grew tense as he saw the crowds.

Just outside the gate, Charlotte and Bert came upon Mr. Smithers talking to an old man dressed in leather and so browned by the sun and wind that he might have been an Indian. This was Ebenezer Hall, Mr. Smithers' old trapping partner.

Mr. Smithers put out a hand to restrain them as they were about to hurry toward the wagon encampment.

"Here they are, Ebenezer!" Mr. Smithers said. "Them

134

plucky folks I told ye about that's travelin' the trail, just them and their ma."

Charlotte bobbed a curtsy, but Moses hissed at the old man.

"Yes, 'Nezer, them and their cat took to the trail, just like they was born to it," Mr. Smithers went on. "And lookee here, 'Nezer! Their cat puts me in mind of that good-luck cat ye and I had, twenty-thirty years back up on the Bear. Little ol' Odd-Eyes. Rec'lect? I don't recall I ever seen an odd-eyed cat since. Have ye, 'Nezer?"

The old man leaned forward, balancing himself on his cane to look at Moses more closely. The cat hissed furiously.

'Nezer Hall chuckled. "Nope, Smitty, don't rec'lect that I ever seen one after our little oddy, until along, oh, say about the first of the season. The factor's cat, she had kits, and one was a spunky white odd-eyed female. Factor figgered there was too many cats around the fort anyhow, so he was fixin' to drop that sassy odd-eyed cat with a sackful o' rocks into the river yonder. But one of them wagoners, he put up sech a fuss, even offerin' to pay the factor real cash money. I ast him if he be sup'stitious about odd eyes and he told me he weren't. Said he didn't take no truck with notions about luck 'n' cats. But he says she puts him in mind of his little gal way back in the States who has an odd-eyed cat, and he'd like to take 'er along fer old times' sake."

Charlotte gasped and looked at Bert. "Was that man's name Van Antwerp?" he asked huskily.

Old 'Nezer brushed aside this interruption impatiently, not to be delayed in his own story. "Lor', I don't ast them emigrants their names. Bad as tryin' to name the stars in the heavens, they're that thick this year. Funny, jumpy little cuss he was, specially when he got excited. Doc—that was his name, I do rec'lect now, for they says to him, 'Hey,' they sez, 'Doc, whatcha want a cat fer, on the Oregon Trail? Aim to raise mountain cats up ahead?' But this Doc, he jest laughed right back at 'em. Couldn't quite make his words come out right. Sort of Dutchy-like, ye might say."

Bert grabbed Charlotte's hand, and they ran toward the wagon to tell Ma that they had indeed heard word of Pa at Fort Laramie.

Charlotte gladly took to the trail next morning and faced the mountains towering ever more threateningly above them, knowing that they were following Pa's wheel tracks. She wondered about the little white odd-eyed cat whose life Pa had saved. Would she be as good a traveler as Moses?

The journey was always uphill now, the mountains never out of sight, range after range of them rolling off into the blue distance. The Warren train did well, with their rickety wagons and tired oxen, to make fifteen miles a day. One day blurred with another until Charlotte wearily gave up trying to record the time on the notched bow of the wagon frame.

A week beyond Fort Laramie they came to their final crossing of the Platte, the North Platte this time. It was all very businesslike with the Mormon ferrymen expertly handling their craft and collecting their tolls: one young animal or one dollar and fifty cents' worth of foodstuffs or three dollars in cash. When Lottie Van Antwerp paid with her last bit of white flour, Charlotte thought wistfully of light, crispy-crusted yeast bread. But she put regrets out of her mind, for each river crossed meant they were that much closer to Pa and Johnny and Oregon.

Once across the Platte, Mrs. Van Antwerp talked one evening at lesson time about the Sweetwater River, along which they would now travel. Inch by tiresome inch, they were coming closer to South Pass in the Rocky Mountains.

"And then," said Mrs. Van Antwerp, "the rivers will be just like us—hurrying westward to the Pacific Ocean, to Oregon!"

They all felt a stir of excitement at her words, all but little Alice, who remained pale and weak after her fever.

Nothing interested her, not even baby Edgar's bouncing, gurgling good health. People shook their heads behind Captain Warren's back. "She'll never make it," they said.

Many long afternoons Charlotte held Alice, singing softly to her until she fell asleep. They were together the day the train approached Independence Rock. It was a late August day on the spot where they should have celebrated the Fourth of July. Alice wakened as they drew into the evening circle before the great mass of rock that looked like a crouching monster. She patted Charlotte's cheek and asked, "Where's kitty? Alice wants to pet kitty!"

"Shh! The kitty's sleeping way back in the other wagon," Charlotte whispered, hoping neither Mrs. Warren nor Lucy had heard Alice's request.

"Kitty!" Alice persisted fretfully.

To distract her Charlotte said, "Look at Independence Rock, Alice. Lots of people have written their names on it. We'll ask Bert and Reuben to put your name on the rock."

After supper Reuben and Bert took the tar pail and brush and climbed up the rock to paint in wobbly letters "Alice + Charlotte" for later travelers to read.

For several days now one idea had filled Captain Warren's mind. If only a doctor could be found, Alice might be saved. Mrs. Van Antwerp had done her best, but it was not enough.

Early that morning Mr. Smithers had saddled the fastest riding horse in the train and left camp before anyone was up. Rumor had it that there was a doctor with the party of emigrants two groups ahead of the Warren train. Perhaps he could be persuaded to come back to look at Alice.

Now as Charlotte pointed to where Alice's name was written in tall letters, the pilot and a stranger rode into camp. The doctor! Everyone's hopes rose.

The men quickly surrounded the newcomers. The doctor did not go directly to the Warren wagon, as Charlotte had supposed he would.

Dr. Cutler brought serious news. A young man in a wagon train ahead had shot at what he thought was an antelope. Instead he had killed an Indian.

Because the Indians might take revenge on any white men they could find, special precautions were necessary. There would be no fires in camp since smoke might attract Indians. Cold supper and early to bed would be the rule this evening. Men were warned under no circumstances to fire their guns. The animals were penned in the circle of the wagons, and a strict guard planned for the night.

As the men scattered to join their families, Dr. Cutler turned his attention to little Alice.

Charlotte and her mother waited with the Warrens to hear the doctor's advice.

"In my opinion," he said, "the little girl has safely survived her illness. Now what ails her is lack of food. She needs something like a rich chicken broth to give her nourishment. She'll regain her strength when she begins to eat."

Mrs. Warren's voice trembled as she answered, "We've tried our best. I can hardly get her to take a mouthful of anything."

"Trail food, that's all we have," Captain Warren interrupted. "Beans and hard biscuits and maybe a bit of salt pork."

"You'll have to do something," the doctor said. "I can't prescribe any medicine except food the child will eat and can digest."

"But what if—?" Captain Warren asked desperately.

There was no answer. The doctor simply shook his head. He had seen much suffering on the trail, but he was still moved by each new tragedy. Now he swung into his saddle and prepared to ride to his own camp.

Captain Warren put his arms around his wife. "We shouldn't have come," he said in a low voice. "The trail costs a man too much. If we were back on our farm in Pennsylvania, Alice would never have had a sick day."

Charlotte said softly to Lucy, "Oh, if only we hadn't lost our chickens! Then Alice could have had eggs and chicken soup, too."

Captain Warren turned suddenly on the girls and demanded, "What are you doing—listening to other people's troubles? Both of you get to bed!"

Charlotte stumbled in the dark to the Van Antwerp wagon. Suddenly she felt something rub against her ankles, then she heard a purring sound.

"Moses!" she whispered, and stopped to stroke him, almost invisible in the darkness.

One moment Charlotte was touching Moses, the next she felt him become alert and slip quickly beyond her grasp. He bounded silently out of the circle of wagons, then crouched where Charlotte could not see him.

Dared she call him? No, there was no use in attracting Captain Warren's attention. She didn't really think there could be Indians out there in the darkness, but the children had been sternly warned to stay by the wagons and not wander farther than the riverbank. Holding her breath, she waited.

There was a rustle—Moses had pounced at something, she was sure. Whatever Moses had stalked was so panicked that it ran against Charlotte, startling her. Charlotte should not have screamed, but she could not help it.

"Who's there?" Captain Warren called in a low yet commanding voice. The quick silence over the camp was tense. Indians! There must be Indians out there. A thin cry came from the Warren wagon—Alice, just drifting into sleep, had been wakened.

"It's—it's me," Charlotte answered in a small, shaking voice. "I'm all right, really I am. It isn't anything."

"Come here," Captain Warren directed. And when Charlotte stood in front of him she could almost feel the heat of his anger. "What do you mean, it isn't anything? You frightened everyone. You woke. my little girl. You didn't scream for nothing. What happened?"

Charlotte had no choice. She had to tell what Moses had done. And to make matters worse, the mischievous little cat padded toward her, tail held high.

"I've told you, Charlotte Van Antwerp," Captain Warren said, "that cat is bad luck and a danger to us all. I've warned you. I won't have any more of this." He raised his gun.

"Stop!" Mr. Smithers said quickly. "You let them savages hear a gunshot tonight and we'll all pay for it."

Nothing softened the anger on Captain Warren's face. "Give me that cat," he demanded. "I'll drown it over yonder."

"No!" Charlotte cried. "If he has to die, I'll drown him myself! Nobody's going to touch him."

"That young'un has spunk," Mr. Smithers said. "Let her take care of it herself."

There was an uneasy stir among the people who had gathered.

"She won't drown him—he'll escape," Mr. Harris said.

"Poor child," Mrs. Alden whispered. "I remember how I loved my kitty—"

"I'll do it!" Charlotte said stubbornly. "Give me a sack and I'll put stones in it. He won't get away. I promise!" Her heart pounded, her hands were cold. Captain Warren thrust a burlap sack and a bit of rope at her. Stooping, she gathered Moses in her arms.

Charlotte sensed both sympathy and disapproval in the group standing in a circle around Captain Warren. She climbed over the wagon tongue to go to the river. Strangely, in her last glimpse of the captain in the moonlight, his face was sad, not angry.

She paused on the riverbank, kneeling to thrust Moses headfirst into the sack. He wriggled free and poked his head through the opening before Charlotte could close it securely with the rope. Then he slipped between her hands and disappeared into the night.

Charlotte crumpled, muffling her sobs in the scratchy burlap. Now she had failed everyone: her promise to the captain, the trust Ma and Pa always had in her. Moses was free, yes, but free to return to camp in the morning only to be shot by the captain.

The silence around Charlotte was smothering. The river made a tiny lapping sound, hardly audible. A breeze rustled the grass. Straining for any sound of Moses, Charlotte heard the cry of an animal taken by surprise. Hardly a sound at all, but a signal.

Then there was Moses, carrying in his mouth the furry animal that this time had not escaped him. He was bringing it to Charlotte to win her attention, as he always did.

Dimly the girl could see the animal was a rabbit, nearly

142

lifeless. It's an answer to a prayer, she thought swiftly. Moving so rapidly that Moses did not resist, she scooped up the cat and the rabbit. Then with fast, light steps she ran toward the circle of wagons.

In the dim moonlight the men waiting near the Warren wagon stared at her. Moses let go of the rabbit and gave an angry hiss.

Captain Warren took Charlotte's arm in a rough grip. "So!" he said. "You're to be trusted, missy?"

"Sir!" Charlotte said. "Look—a rabbit! Rabbit broth for Alice! It's almost as good as chicken."

That name—Alice—stopped Captain Warren as nothing else could have done. Charlotte seized the opportunity and thrust the rabbit into his hand. "Ma can cook it," she said.

Mrs. Van Antwerp stepped toward the captain. "Give me the rabbit. I'll make a fire in a trench so nothing's to be seen. There'll be broth for Alice tomorrow, ready when she wakes."

Captain Warren gave Mrs. Van Antwerp the rabbit. "Get to bed—you and your cat, too," he said roughly to Charlotte. But it wasn't the tone he had used before, and Charlotte felt relief surge over her. Holding Moses so close that he threatened to scratch, she did not wait to say goodnight.

Next morning at dawn as the camp stirred and prepared to move, Mrs. Van Antwerp, with Charlotte following, carried to the Warren wagon a steaming cup of rabbit broth with a few tiny shreds of meat.

Mrs. Warren, with Alice on her lap, reached eagerly for the cup. "Here, honey," she crooned. "See what Charlotte has for her little girl. Doesn't it smell good? Have a sip."

And as Captain Warren watched, the miracle happened.

144

Alice took a spoonful, another, and another. "Good!" she said.

"There's more left to have later," Mrs. Van Antwerp said. "Come, Charlotte, let's get packed."

Mr. Smithers was already urging an early start. The summer was waning and the mountains lay ahead. There was not an hour to waste. "You'll catch mice—and rabbits, too—in Oregon!" Charlotte told Moses as she hugged him. And this time she made the promise with new confidence.

How far away the woods of Wisconsin seemed, and the flat Kansas and Nebraska prairies! For nearly a thousand miles the Warren train had rolled along, and still a thousand miles to be traveled before the haven of the Willamette Valley.

South Pass was so broad and gentle that it hardly seemed to Charlotte the famous gateway through the Rockies. At Pacific Creek the wagons came to a halt. Men and women jumped down from wagon seats or slid off their horses. They dipped their hands in the cold mountain water: it was flowing to Oregon, to the Pacific! Charlotte joined in the cheers.

That night around the campfire Mr. Sawyer tuned his fiddle, and many of the young couples joined in a square dance. Even Captain Warren took a turn with Mrs. Warren. To the delighted surprise of everyone, Mr. Smithers kicked up his heels in a Highland fling. Alice, almost her healthy self again, laughed and clapped to the sound of the violin.

From South Pass the travelers turned into Sublette's Cut-off. It presented a new hazard. The trail crossed hot, alkali desert where pools of poisoned water were sure death to the animals.

Mr. Smithers outlined the plan most emigrants used. They would rest in the daytime and travel by night. Although the peak of summer was past, the sun could be a

146

burning, blinding danger to anyone plodding across those dry miles by day.

As the Van Antwerp wagon fell into line for the first night march Charlotte asked, "Ma, do you suppose Pa and Johnny came this way?"

"I expect they did," Ma said. "They should be in Oregon right this minute."

Looking up at the stars bright in the dark sky, Charlotte said, "But it's all so big and we're so little. How will we ever find Pa and Johnny?"

"Don't fret," her mother answered. "We haven't come all this way to worry about that now. We'll find them, never you fear."

Charlotte was silent for a time, then she said, "I have a funny feeling that maybe Pa and John aren't so far off after all. Anyway it makes me feel good to think that."

"And maybe you're right," Ma said. "Who knows?"

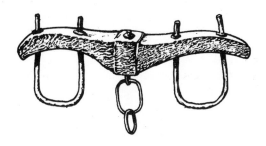

To everyone the desert looked ghostly and forbidding at night. They were relieved when this part of the journey was behind them and the wagons were ferried across the Green River.

The emigrants followed the Bear River, bordered by grassy meadowlands. The animals, thin and weary from rough desert country, grazed eagerly. The women and children picked berries, and some of the men went hunting and fishing. If only the season were not so late, Bert said, they'd stay longer.

Where earlier trains had lingered, the Warren train hurried on, pushed always by the fear of autumn snows in the high mountains. The marvels of Soda Springs and then Steamboat Springs paled before the cold reality of light frost each morning.

But when they reached the American Falls of the Snake River on the last day of August Mr. Smithers urged that they rest a day or two. Here the Indians caught fish and bartered them for whatever the travelers had to offer. A supplement to dwindling food supplies was welcome indeed.

Free of duties, Charlotte set out to explore around the falls, running after Moses as he frisked along. She found, however, that she soon had to drop down on the riverbank to rest. Now that she no longer feared that Captain Warren would harm Moses she was not worried when her pet disappeared from sight.

Suddenly Charlotte heard an outcry of Indian voices mingled with the hissing and spitting of a cat. She and almost everyone in the camp rushed to the spot below the falls where the fishermen were at work.

But for the wrath on the face and in the voice of the Indian standing there, Charlotte would have laughed. The angry chief was handsomely bedecked in finery that members of the Warren train had given up.

Earlier in the day Captain Warren had traded his tall black silk hat for enough fish to feed his family. That silk hat had been tenderly packed and guarded all the way from the East, for Captain Warren had hoped that in Oregon he might become a senator, perhaps a governor. Then a black silk hat would be an impressive touch. Now with Oregon still many hundreds of miles away and with a hungry family to feed, the captain parted with the hat. The chief wore it, clapped firmly on his head.

Mr. Johnson, his mouth watering at the sight of the fish, had traded his Sunday vest and his deacon's cutaway coat for a plump fish for supper. These garments, too, the chief wore—these and nothing else besides his breechcloth.

Standing at the water's edge, the Indian held the spitting cat in one hand and his fish-skinning knife in the other. His little girl, not much bigger than Alice Warren, displayed a partly eaten fish, obviously Moses' work.

As the chief was about to plunge the knife into Moses' throat Charlotte ran forward and snatched the cat from his hands.

"No! No!" she shrieked. "You can't kill him!"

The Indian turned a wrathful look on Charlotte. She bravely stood her ground, clutching Moses. When she saw the horrified glance Mr. Smithers gave her as he came running up she thought her heart would stop. Her mother, pale with anxiety, followed close behind the old guide.

Mr. Smithers spoke to the chief in his own language and the man grew calmer. But the Indian replied in a long and forceful speech of his own.

Shaking his head, Mr. Smithers turned to Charlotte. "He says, missy, that your cat's a thief and oughter be punished."

Charlotte gulped. "Tell the chief—tell his majesty—" she said, groping for placating words, "tell him I don't think Moses was being a thief—he was just—just being a cat!"

The old guide interpreted her words to the Indian. The chief turned from him to look at Charlotte. The anger left his eyes, and after a moment he laughed shortly and spoke again.

"The chief says you're a right smart young'un," Mr. Smithers said. "But he reminds ye that in bein' just a cat Moses stole and spoiled his fish."

"I—I know it," Charlotte said. "Please tell his majesty that I'm sorry and I'll try to pay him for it."

She waited anxiously while Mr. Smithers and the chief talked.

"You've really rubbed his fur the right way with this 'yer majesty' business, missy," Mr. Smithers said. "But he says the fish was his best catch of the day and that he was fixin' to make a feast for his little daughter."

"I'll try to pay," Charlotte pleaded.

Just then the little girl dropped the fish and ran to peer at Moses. She said something to her father, and he bent closer to examine Moses and then talked in an excited manner to Mr. Smithers.

"He says, missy," the guide said, "that your cat must have much magic in him, with them odd eyes, and so if you'll give the cat to him, he'll forgive his stealin' the best fish."

Charlotte thought her heart would break. Moses had survived Captain Warren's anger only to be lost to an Indian! With the eyes of the chief upon her and the worried glances of all her friends, she knew she must not cry. Impulsively she stepped forward, holding out the cat to the Indian as she spoke.

"Tell him I think the magic in Moses turned bad and makes him scratch and bite all men. But if he wants to risk it, I—I suppose he has a right to take him."

True to his mistress' words, Moses lashed out with his

150

claws as he was thrust near the Indian.

The man jumped back to a safe distance. He looked at Charlotte with admiration. He spoke then at great length to Mr. Smithers.

Mr. Smithers turned pale, took off his battered hat, and rubbed his head thoughtfully before he translated.

"He says, Miss Charlotte, that you are the wisest female he has ever known. He says that with your hair the color of moonlight you have even greater magic than your odd-eyed cat and so he'll take you in exchange for the damage your cat has done."

An angry murmur swept across the emigrants, but Mr. Smithers held up his hand to check it. "Guard your feelings, folks," he warned. "He's in a purty ugly mood. For some reason he was settin' great stock by that fish. He dotes on that little girl o' his, and he gives her the best of every catch. Her mother has been dead a long time now, and he thinks Miss Moonlight Magic-Hair here will make the best stepmother in creation fer his little girl."

Lottie Van Antwerp pressed her hand over her mouth and wept. Bert pushed his way through the crowd. He put his arm gently around his mother's shoulders, then stepped forward to stand beside Mr. Smithers. He unfastened Dr. Johan's watch from his pocket. He opened the gold watch. He studied its face and squinted at the sun before he turned to the guide.

"Tell him—tell his majesty," Bert said grandly, "that her moonlight magic has gone sour like the cat's has. Go on, tell him!"

Quickly Mr. Smithers translated Bert's words. The chief listened with interest, watching Bert's face and the gold watch gleaming in his hand.

151

"Tell him in case he doesn't know," Bert went on, "that a female whose magic has gone sour's even worse than a cat whose magic has gone sour."

"Bert Van Antwerp!" Charlotte exclaimed, panic giving a harsh shrillness to her voice. "How dare you go back on me right when I need you most?" She ran to her brother and shook his arm. "Please, please, Bert!"

"Tell him he can see what I mean," Bert said, calmly ignoring his sister.

The Indian, eyeing Charlotte with less admiration now, nodded as Mr. Smithers interpreted.

"Now tell him," said Bert, "that he looks mighty handsome in those clothes, but tell him one thing is missing. That's a nice gold watch to fit into the watch pocket in his vest. Show him where."

Bert stood dangling Pa's watch by the chain while Mr. Smithers spoke and pointed out the empty watch pocket.

"Tell him that he can take Charlotte in payment for the fish—I agree that he deserves payment," Bert said. "But tell him that if he doesn't want to risk a female gone sour I'll buy her back, paying him the watch to go in his pocket."

"Bert! Bert!" Charlotte screamed then. "You mustn't give Pa's watch away!"

"Ye'd jest better hush up, missy," Mr. Smithers said threateningly as he turned to interpret Bert's offer.

The Indian, who had been viewing Charlotte with growing distaste, reached out for the watch. Without needing anyone to interpret, Bert showed the chief how to open and close the watch, how to wind it, and how to use it as a compass. He helped the man fasten it in his empty vest pocket. After that, Bert and the Indian and Mr. Smithers shook hands.

152

Then Bert took Charlotte by one arm and his mother by one arm and with a dignity that was strangely like Pa's he walked to their wagon. The Warren group followed them silently, all sobered by the narrow escape. As they walked Charlotte could feel through Bert's hand on her arm how he was shaking.

When the boy reached the wagon he plunged inside and threw himself across the bedroll, his face hidden.

His mother stayed only briefly and patted his shoulder. "I'm endlessly proud of you, son," she said.

Charlotte, still trembling, sat by her brother and rocked Moses. When Bert sat up she said softly, "Bert, will you ever, ever forgive me for losing you Pa's watch?"

"Oh, Sharlie, Sharlie!" Bert said. "The watch was just doing what Pa told me it'd do—serving us well—but I was so scared that I'd mix things up and say the wrong thing and spoil it all and lose you forever that I'm still shaking all over."

They hugged for a moment before they joined their mother, who was packing the camp equipment.

Immediately after lunch the Warren party set forth on the first lap of the dangerous trip across the Snake River Desert, the part of the trail that had brought suffering to all who had gone before, and death to many.

Everyone took his place in the line of march, hushed by the dangers ahead and still shaken by the danger that had threatened Charlotte. She soothed her little cat, grateful that no one suggested she do away with him. She realized that he had become as much a part of the train as anyone.

The thirsty days crossing the desert of the Snake were probably the strangest ones the emigrants ever spent. The sound of the river roaring endlessly toward its union with the Columbia was always in their ears, for the Snake flowed deep in a canyon whose unscalable walls were of frightening height.

At one place, when everyone was parched for water, Reuben and Bert let themselves down to the river on ropes. They brought back one small pail of water for the women and children. But the way was so steep and rough that Mr. Smithers and Captain Warren forbade any such risk of life again.

Only Moses remained playful among the weary, thirsty travelers. The scanty dew each night seemed to satisfy his thirst. His capers helped Charlotte through the difficult days.

At lesson time around the campfire Ma read to the children from the *Emigrants' Guide to the Oregon Trail,* one of Captain Warren's books.

They'd already passed Fort Hall, and soon they'd come to Fort Boise. Then at last the steep ridges of the Blue Mountains would loom ahead.

The oxen and horses looked like shadows of the fine animals that had stepped out briskly from St. Joseph five months ago. Charlotte and her mother both walked most

of each day through the mountains to make the load the oxen pulled a little lighter. Food was running short, and everyone knew that emigrants of a decade earlier had nearly starved as they passed through this country.

The lovely Grande Ronde Valley was a camping place beyond the Snake River Desert that Charlotte would never forget. Tim and Tuck had pulled the battered wagon faithfully over so many miles. Here Tuck staggered and sank to his knees, never to rise again.

Charlotte and Bert and Ma stood speechless at this tragedy. They grieved for Tuck, and they wondered how they could travel on. Tim for all his endurance could not pull the wagon alone.

"If we had horses," Ma said, "I'd abandon the wagon and ride on to The Dalles. It's maybe a hundred and seventy-five miles from here and we could do it."

"Why don't you hitch up the little cow?" suggested Mr. Smithers. "I've seen worse matched teams along the trail."

The Turner girls will have a time teasing us, Charlotte thought to herself, for the cow and the ox made a strange looking team.

No one, however, had the heart even to smile at some of the makeshift measures that had to be adopted. The families of the wagon train had been through too much together, and now the end of the trail was not so far off. Once they had believed it would never come. Now if they could cross these final miles to the Columbia River, the land of their dreams would be in sight.

15 Occasionally the Warren train met riders on horseback headed east. It was October now and sometimes there was a chance to exchange news. The last days through the mountains had luckily been free of snow, but they dared not pause long at any stop. They pushed toward The Dalles, on the Columbia River.

As they plodded onward, onward, the wind felt colder each day.

"It'll snow anytime now, and we'll all freeze to death before we get there," Essie Turner predicted one cold morning.

Charlotte wished that Essie would not always be so gloomy. "October's early for snow," she suggested. "Don't you think we just feel colder watching Mt. Hood, all covered with snow?"

But one morning, everyone awoke to find that Essie's gloomy prediction had come true. The camp was covered with two inches of snow. Panic reigned, although Mr. Smithers told the travelers cheerily, "Shucks! Don't let this worry ye. This is just poor man's fertilizer. Be gone in no time at all. I'm lookin' for a nice, warm chinook wind to come blowin' from beyond Mt. Hood any minute."

And he was right. By noon, that strange gentle wind of the Pacific, the chinook, warmed them and melted the snow.

"Your folks going on by wagon or flatboat?" Charlotte asked Lucy the day before they reached the settlement.

156

"Pa thinks that with Edgar and Alice and all, we're best going on by wagon. What about you?" Lucy asked.

"Ma and Bert talk about getting passage on a flatboat," Charlotte said. "I don't know what kind of sailors Moses and I'll make."

Essie said, "Ooh, I wouldn't like that. They say the Columbia is a terrible treacherous river. Them flatboats sink mighty easy."

"Well, I don't guess Tim and Daisy can travel many more miles," Charlotte said. "Ma'll have to decide."

With a feeling of victory in spite of her weariness, Charlotte peered ahead as the wagon at last pulled into the little village of The Dalles. Soon she and Ma and Bert would reach the Willamette Valley, the rich promised land of her father's dreams.

Ma found a camping spot at the edge of the village, nestled on a shelf of land at the river's edge.

"Bert, you come with me," she said. "I'm going to buy us some food and see what I can do about passage on a boat downriver. Charlotte, you stay here and mind the camp. Lots of strangers here in this town. Don't know when we've seen so many people since we left Fort Laramie."

"What about Pa?" Charlotte asked. "Suppose there's some news here?"

"If there's anything to learn, Ma'll learn it," Bert said. "You stay here, Sharlie. We'll bring the news back."

Charlotte felt pushed aside even though she realized someone had to stay with the wagon. She scooped up Moses and scratched his head until he purred. "I just wish I could be the one to hear the news," she said. "Maybe you and I'll just explore a little bit and see what we can see."

Something urged Charlotte along the river. She passed

other wagons camped like her own, but shyness kept her from speaking to anyone.

"We'd better go back," Charlotte told Moses. "If Ma and Bert find us gone—"

Moses suddenly gathered himself into a coiled spring and leaped from her arms with startling speed.

"Moses!" she cried. And then she saw Moses streaking toward something white. It couldn't be a white rabbit. What was it?

Charlotte gathered up her tattered skirts and chased after her little black cat. She hadn't fought to bring him all these hundreds and hundreds of miles to lose him now!

The white animal stopped and turned on Moses. It was a white cat, almost his twin in size. Its tail was fluffed out, its back arched, and its eyes blazed.

A white cat? Something teased at Charlotte's mind, but she was intent on catching Moses.

"Here kitty, kitty!" she coaxed.

Suddenly a man stepped in the path and picked up the white cat—not roughly, but with the skill of someone who handles live creatures.

"You like cats, too?" he asked Charlotte, who was stooping to retrieve Moses. "My daughter . . ."

"Pa!" Charlotte cried. "Pa, it's you, it's you!" She rushed toward the short man cradling the white cat.

For an instant he looked uncomprehending, then he cried, "Sharlie! My own Sharlie-girl!"

The white cat slipped from his hold and Moses escaped from Charlotte. Strong arms were around her, her father's beard tickled her forehead.

"You're here!" Dr. Van Antwerp said. "Mamma and Bert—where are they?"

"Oh, come!" Charlotte cried. "We're all here!" Together the father and daughter hurried along the path toward the Van Antwerp wagon. Breathlessly, Charlotte filled in a few details about how they had come and why.

Just as they reached the wagon, Ma and Bert came up, arms filled with their purchases.

At first Charlotte thought her mother was going to faint. She stared at her husband as if she believed him a ghost. Then he held her, tears streaming down both their faces. Charlotte and Bert hugged each other just for good measure.

For a time everyone talked at once, or so it seemed. Dr. Van Antwerp had been at The Dalles for nearly three weeks, awaiting the birth of the pastor's child in his own train. Johnny, however, had gone on to the Willamette Valley. Only two days ago he had sent back word of good luck.

"Listen, my dears," Pa said, and he unfolded a letter and read, " 'I have found a farm for us. The owner who built the house and barn wants to move his family to California. As soon as weather permits in the spring, if you agree, I will go for Ma, Charlotte, and Bert. Your son, John.' "

"Wonderful, wonderful!" Charlotte chanted. "Only here we are! How soon can we go?"

"We'll take flatboat passage together," her father answered, "as soon as we can book it."

Just then two shadows slipped quietly toward the campfire. Charlotte scooped up Moses, and Dr. Van Antwerp swept up the white cat.

"Look, Ma!" Charlotte said. "I almost forgot—it was Moses who found Pa and his kitty! Now we'll have two cats for our new farm."

"And maybe more!" Ma said.